ATTENTION SCAN

JONATHAN WYMER
&
JOSHUA MESSARGE

Attention Scan Vol 1
Copyright © 2020 by Jonathan Wymer & Joshua Messarge

Cover design by Joshua Messarge & Jonathan Wymer

First Edition

ISBN: 978-0-578-77442-8

To Lisa, whose love and kindness is from another dimension.
-JW

For Inez Prescott (Nauna)
-JM

PREFACE

Growing up in the tail-end of the Postmodern Era, it can be difficult to understand where we are headed as a species entering the Disinformation Era. But there are moments when stories arise from the sea of convoluted messages and must be told. Attention Scan was first written as a standalone short story birthed out of malcontent for the undiscernible amount of entertainment and information we're fed today. From that small story began a journey in deciphering the code of ethics and consequences involved with feeding conglomerates with our undivided attention.

When we chose to expand on the short story, originally meant to be a simplistic narrative within the genre of science fiction, we immediately recognized the irony in that venture. And so, we chose the appropriate writing technique for the expansion of such a story where our personal feelings and experiences could be filtered into a compelling, extended world of stories. Stream of Consciousness is that technique. This style of writing gave us the freedom and focus needed for our story to be truthful and sincere in its telling. This became the foundation for the novel you now hold in your hands.

The characters and their stories herein are a work of fiction, but the feelings and conflict they experience are as true as what we as writers felt in the moments of its fragmented realization. The process of writing Attention Scan was an experiment that was tried and tested in the organic conversations we had concerning its creation. It was an unforgettable experience that we hope others will share while reading the stories of our characters. And our hope is that through their stories, you discover the truth resting behind the veil of your own unique perspective. Because within this book, there are...

...Stories for all of us.

VOLUME ONE

Stories for all of us

EPISODE 1

The last time I saw the sky, the Cloud did not exist and I was eight years old. I could feel the warm air rise up from the pavement and grace my neck; the fumes unbearable. There wasn't a sign of nature outside of the wind, the sky, and the sun. The moon has been gone awhile. Looking up from the ground I could see-

"That's enough for today," he said. The doctor spun around in his tilted swivel chair, which I'm sure was manufactured at the same plant my mother worked at before she passed; I recognize the design. It fit the décor for the rest of the doctor's exam room: bland, colorless, procedural. And I realize now that my perspective on this style of interior decorating amused me in its level of ironic control. Afterall, I live in a world that harvests imagination, investigates ideas, and tries to pinpoint interests and motivations through the mind. *Shit.* He hasn't paused the scanning yet.

I heard the wheels of his small chair squeak as he came into view and blocked my angle on the ceiling. His cigarette-stained canines and patchy stubble were the first features I noticed before he spoke, as always. "You know, Clarice… Your mother would be excited to learn that something she made was put to good use," he chuckled while prodding the thought of her and seeming to make a double entendre at the same time. And I continued to see her charcoaled skin flash before me as she gave me a sullen stare.

I tried to make my mind blank, but that would show up on his monitor, too. It didn't help that I had to bear the pneumatic sound of the doctor adjusting the chair higher to remove the scanning helmet. "And so is your imagination," he continued. "We're making good progress and your collection of thoughts is growing. I know it must be difficult, being sixteen and working in the plant. But try to keep your thoughts positive, Clarice." He turned off the scanner.

Oh, I will stay positive all right. I will work harder to control my thoughts, too. Because I know what will happen to me if I don't.

YEAR: 2032   **DAY: 34 of 231**

EPISODE 2

I felt a tick somewhere in the back of my mind that would not cease. Something that required my full attention to solve its purpose. It seemed to plague me with doubts and fears. Why? Something is wrong. I can hardly concentrate anymore. I feel divided. What came before this ticking? Oh! That's right! I'm remembering. A new discovery.

"This formula can completely revolutionize the Cloud, Laura. It'll be incredible! It should eliminate any concerns people still have toward it, and we can finally connect everyone together into the next generation of the Cloud! Laura? Laura, are you listening?" She stood there swiping the air with her hand as the wall cycled through various shades of blue. "Laura?" I dropped onto the beige, flower-printed couch.

"What are you doing, Theo?" She finally said, still not looking at me. "The movers will be here any moment to delete it and install the new one."

Shit. I forgot all about the movers, or did she even tell me about them? I don't remember. The tick resurfaced. "Why are we getting rid of it? It's been in my family for generations."

"It's old. I'd like to get a new one. We discussed this already." Her words landed with impact. That was that. The end of our discussion on the topic. "What about this shade? It feels pleasant, doesn't it?" She said.

It was a sickly teal. "Sure," I said, ending that discussion too.

I picked up my keys and my notebook, which contained the mathematical equation of the discovery, and headed out the door to catch the bus to work. I couldn't bear to wait around and watch the couch deleted and discarded so thoughtlessly. I hated even dwelling on the idea. Something that held value once, even still. No matter, I was running late and removed the sadden thought from my mind.

YEAR: 2032   **DAY: 34 of 231**

EPISODE 3

There is a hand that strikes me whenever the moon is full and I do not know why. And the feeling of dread before the hand delivers its blow to my cheek is unbearable. Black and white. Black and white. The image burns, sending shivers down my spine and goosebumps appear with each ray of light that illuminates this memory… Where am I?

Identity can be found in touch. A newborn baby knows its mother's touch better than any other surface it comes in contact with. This sensation is numbed out of existence with my daily routine. Before entering my apartment, a digital scan of my palm. It's irritating, almost searing my flesh with each small dose of radiation that pulses between the screen and my hand. There's also the sound of my wall television output. A snarky sitcom belting out irrevocable cynicisms that are meant to provide some form of comfort in these times.

These times. What are these times, anyway? Entering my apartment, I'm plagued with the provocations of the continuing sitcom while trying to compartmentalize each passing thought. The dish towel draping the pull bar on the stove, the closest I'll ever get to a mother's touch again. I inherited this place when she died. It's something I've been thinking about more and more as each day comes to a close, and the scanning has been the prime usurper of this trying behavior. What was that thought I had while in the scanning chair? I was outside, I remember that. The hot pavement under my feet. I'm now remembering that I wore sandals. And I'm remembering. Is this a thought of the past, then? It couldn't possibly be the present. There is no wind in the city anymore.

A smudge on the window. This sort of distraction deserves my full attention. And so, I sway my hand in a fluid composer-like motion to turn off the wall television. Nothing is ever out of place in my apartment. It's possibly a nervous tick of mine, or worst, a mental disorder issued by the State for scanning purposes. The wall television turns off but it will return. In the city, the citizens are required to have a minimum of six hours of televised programming per day. This sort of mandate brings about no rebellion as it gives validity to most of the city's non-working social class. The smudge on the window... What could it be?

YEAR: 2032   *DAY: 34 of 231*

EPISODE 4

A gaudy advertisement played on the teleprompter outside my low-rise apartment building. A prodigious crowd had gathered, waiting to be tantalized by the showcase of estate homes that flashed on screen. The installation of them was coming soon. These homes boasted an array of technological advancements for easy comfortable living; endless amenities, luxurious projected views, and, seemingly, any self-indulgent request one could imagine. It was the kind of fantasy lifestyle one could hope to obtain. It was also an extravagance one could afford while working for Cloud Tech; one of the most prestigious companies, and one of the last.

I pushed through the statically fixated crowd just in time and caught the bus before it pulled away. Taking a seat in the back, I scoured through my notes again performing the mental equation over and over. It had to be foolproof for the theory to work as planned. If I was even one decimal point off there could be grave consequences. However, I couldn't concentrate. The advertisement continued on portable screens fixed-in each seatback. The bus stopped again, picking up more passengers.

"Theo! Theo! Have you seen the news? Did you hear what's happening today?" My friend Lyle, a short, plump fellow with a severe case of rosacea, hastily took the seat next to me and without even catching his breath he continued, "They're calling you up! What do you think about that? Oh, boy! I bet they're giving you one of the new estate homes! Have you seen them? They're beautiful, aren't they? Gee! You must be ecstatic, huh?"

I've put in ten strong years with the company, having been brought on for an internship at seventeen and climbing the ranks rapidly within it. Now, I currently lead an engineer team. There had been numerous occasions I've worked over-time, patching updates for the Cloud, and I was part of the team that reimagined and expertly navigated the Cloud's technology into the public's hands making it more accessible. Yet, I felt a sense of dread. I was too young. *It must be some mistake*, I thought. For a moment, the screen flickered with white static lines, an indiscernible image flashed behind it, then returned to normal broadcasting. "Where did you hear that rumor?" I said.

"Why, everyone knows about it in the office. You haven't heard about it on your floor? Strange."

The *tick* prodded at the back of my skull. Whatever was bound for me I would soon find out. Still, I can't remember ever knowing anyone who's been called up. I'm sure this was a mistake. A misunderstanding. I couldn't shake the lurking fear.

YEAR: 2032   **DAY: 34 of 231**

EPISODE 5

They've said the last thing they would replace would be the oxygen. Finding alternate sources are their bread and butter, and there's no way to turn back and reverse the necessities they've engineered artificially. I imagine an escape from this assembly line of fatal attraction to something deemed by higher authorities to be more pretty, more put-together, perfect. I almost think – SHIT. I almost thought.

I stepped out onto the hot pavement outside my apartment entrance. The sun was bright and so harsh that it gave me a slight headache. There was a foul smell nearby. My email box still says *Clarice Richardson*, but almost no one goes by first and last names these days. And the avatar displayed just below the projection is still me as an eight-year-old. That's postmodern technology for you. Most of this tech won't ever receive an upgrade due to their primary focus: The Cloud.

I noticed this lack of an update when I came outside for a much-needed smoke. Somehow not only does the nicotine help me focus, but it gives me a sensation of control. An equilibrium to my lonely world is inhaled in and projected out into small rings of smoke. It helps me think, too. And I love it.

I still questioned the smudge on my sliding glass door.

Still wondered how anything could reach it from the tenth floor. And it's not like there's anything still in the sky to…

And that's when I noticed the bird. A cardinal. Its size seeming larger than normal since I haven't seen a bird ever in my life; and the fact that the bird's wings are fully expanded at maximum wingspan. Its ruffled feathers coating a lifeless body that showed signs of a cruel death, and possibly a death with a certain height of falling and landing. There probably isn't a person alive in this world right now that has seen a bird. It seems like a form of conspiracy, and my elevated heart rate would suggest that I'm worried that someone else might see it now. My primal instinct kicks in, or at least it feels primal. My thoughts have felt somewhat manipulated lately. Or it could just be the cigarette. I've got to hide the bird.

YEAR: 2032   **DAY: 34 of 231**

EPISODE 6

Tick... Tick... Tick... Tick... Tick... Tick... Tick...
The future is unavoidable. Cruelly, it waits for us all, bringing forth light and darkness. Time is not the enemy though. It simply issues us the reminder of inevitability, of outcome, of fate. The provocateur of what is unknowable. The true enemy is the self-proclaimed who manipulates these events, dictating by edict what it holds for us all.
Tick... Tick... Tick... Tick... Tick... Tick... Tick...

In the laboratory where I conduct my work, we have wall clocks. These relentlessly *ticking* clocks, which provide us with the exact time of every country, every major city, and even of distant uninhabited planets, completely surround us in the circular, sterile room. They never stop running. They're always exact.

Today, every passing second landed with the suffocating blow of an arrow into my skull. No one in the laboratory had heard of a request of me being called up. Maybe it wasn't true?

The day ran normally when I arrived. As lead engineer of group #77, which consists of only four of us, we are tasked to conduct improvements to the scanning helmet. However,

I had to know if the formula Raymond and I discovered was correct. I entered it into the computing device and hit enter, watching the green numbers scramble to a conclusion. I didn't hear the door open or even Raymond behind me until I felt the cold grip of his hand dig into my shoulder. He immediately pulled the cords from the processor before the final result showed. "We were wrong, all wrong. It must all be deleted. Everything we've discovered. All proof of it. *Keep nothing, Theo*." He whispered gravely.

"Contamination!" Shouted one of the engineers. I turned, seeing a small black speck with a yellow back traveling through the air; a *fly*. One of the engineers quickly rose with a neutralizing-spray and sent a plume of mist in its direction. It dropped by the door and was crushed under a polished black shoe where a tall and slender suited man had entered. Slowly, his emotionless features scanned the room behind dark sunglasses. His gaze landed on me. He spoke coolly, "Theodore Brimley. They are ready to see you now. Please, follow me."

Tick... Tick... Tick... Tick... Tick... Tick... Tick...

The future is unavoidable.
Cruelly, it waits for us all, bringing forth light and darkness.
Time is not the enemy though.
It simply issues us the reminder of inevitability, of outcome, of fate.
The provocateur of what is unknowable.
The wall clocks had all stopped ticking.

...   **...**   **...**   **...**   **...**   **...**   **...**

YEAR: 2032   **DAY: 34 of 231**

EPISODE 7

It's one-way glass and yet both sides can be seen through prayer and supplication. The man in the monster suit screams loud through speakers but a silent avant-garde picture says more to our morality than the trumpets that blare at rapture. I see, I hear, and my mouth says nothing.

Back in my apartment, I couldn't help but notice the automated television compulsion. It turned back on without my consent and I felt immediately plugged in. That rush of energy that you'd get from a caffeinated drink or the adrenaline exploding and crashing like an adolescent go-kart race in your veins is injected and disbursed at such a rapid pace that your heart begins to tighten and loosen all at once. Critical thinking takes a backseat. I felt this, but it was not my feeling that bothered me.

The program on TV was something related to the archetypal postmodern family in a world where mowing the lawn and squeezing oranges through a serrated juicer was not only the norm, but it was expected. Was this the informercial or the original narrative with structure and characters? I didn't have time to find the answer as the light flickered in and out in subtle gesture that made me quickly dart my attention back to the sliding glass door, looking past the smudge, and realizing that the sun had set. I never will get used to how dark it gets when the sun sets. No moon, no stars, and no questioning or hypothesizing about what lies in the great beyond above our minds. Only a great black abyss that is opposite of our world. And that's when I feel a sense of convulsions coming on. A potential seizure, or at least the thought of it, and I'm then frozen in fear of not being able to control my body and fight the automated protection against itself. The TV and I somehow had become close friends in that moment.

I saw a character on the television acting the part of a tired father coming home from work. He reminded me of my own father, except the memories of him are blurry, dark, and give off a vibe of unpleasantness. I don't want to think about it. So, I yawn, both mimicking the father character and realizing I'm also growing weary. I look down on the counter to see the cardinal I brought in from the scorching late afternoon heat, and we both sit there in the battle between the dark and flashing light of the shimmering televised life force, one alive and one dead. And there's a note tied to the lifeless, to its leg. My very own crimson homing pigeon. And I thought the red on my hands was blood, but in fact it was paint.

YEAR: 2032   **DAY: 34 of 231**

EPISODE 8

Laura. I missed her. I missed the old her. Flashes of her tawny chestnut hair spooled through my memories. The imperfections of budding blackheads on her face that she carefully concealed with makeup before leaving our apartment. The gentle smell of the perfume she always wore, lavender and coconut. Yes, I missed the old her. In those days, it was easy to talk the time away without a care in the world, dream together of the future without distractions, and spend the day in loving embrace because we were young and foolish and in love. But now, those days felt so far removed. They exist only as remnants and memories, like the great Egyptian pyramids that were built as religious tombs for their pharaohs, or of the Aztec temples built to get closer to the gods.

I was claustrophobic in the gold-plated elevator that rose slowly to the upmost floor. The suited man never uttered a word the entire way. My heart raced with panic and fear. I felt I was in my own tomb already. This gold-plated cage ascended to my final judgement where I was to be deemed by *higher authority* of… What? Desperately, all I wanted was to hear Laura's tender voice again. It was the only thought I could conjure that gave me any will at all in that moment. A strength and vitality that made me feel youthful again. Capable of *anything*.

I thought of the great Egyptian pyramids that were built under dogmatic reverence to an afterlife for their pharaohs. I thought of the Aztec temples, *Teocalli* as called by their people, that were god houses used for worship and offerings. I thought of the Cloud which was the new reign of civilizations combining merit. This technological booming infrastructure would connect all of us together by *ideas*, by information, and by shared human experiences. It was supposed to be a good thing. *Was?* Was it not?

I missed the old Laura. The distance between us was becoming greater and more evident with each passing day. In the age of transparency, through the progress of technology, we were slowly becoming extinct. The artifacts of us remained only in memories now. If I saw her again, if I held her again, I would not let us be so easily destroyed. I would fight to reclaim what we built together.

The elevator doors opened, and a dark, narrow corridor laid in front of me.

YEAR: 2032   **DAY: 34 of 231**

EPISODE 9

Enter the cage to be free from it…

The screen of the television went dark, and so did the room. The blood, or paint, of the bird sent fumes up my nostrils that procured an alert state of mind. The silence was as loud as the roaring train system underneath our feet in the heart of the city. I could feel my blood pulsing through every vein, my heart working hard in compensation for lack of breath. I had the note in my hand.

It was parchment, which I couldn't help but wonder how it existed. The note was dipped in a lubricant meant to preserve it and solidify the purple ink that graced its face. I noticed the handwriting as I unraveled it further. My father's. The screensaver on the television ignited, a full moon rising from the lower corner of the projected glass. If shivers were meant as a warning sign from our bodies, I certainly feel that urgency now. But I stilled myself to read it: *Enter the cage to be from it…*

My thoughts ran through a mental concourse on their own. And that worried me. Something has tapped into me. The tingling you get when you know someone is watching you from a dark corner in the room, the dread that comes with the decision to turn around or not. My heart started to ache from the adrenaline. And it also ached from the memory that clung to me like the painted blood from this bird. A red stain on my black heart that never found forgiveness to gift my abusive father. His handwriting, his parchment, and his hand that struck me.

Ding, ding! The fairy bells ringing from every device in my apartment. A notification. It pops up on the television and read aloud by the AI inherent to a security system. "Building has been breached by law enforcement. Building has been breached by law enforcement. Remain calm and cooperate." The perspective of a security camera was all I needed to know the extent of this invasion. It was then that I watched dozens of invaders in bullet proof vests, helmets, and protective Kevlar stained in the government's insignia, a blue Monarch butterfly, storm the hallways inside my apartment building. The words from the note burning in my head: *Enter the cage to be from it…*

I stopped thinking. I chose to act. Because at that moment, I felt automated, controlled, governed by an outside influence that had been there all along. I don't know why I felt like their thief, their criminal. It was the most natural feeling in the world and I had to rebel. I slid into my bedroom, grabbed a duffle bag, packed necessities, wasn't picky in the slightest. I kept the note, I clung to it like every word written on it clung to my mind. Pausing after I opened the sliding glass door, I buffed out the smudge with my shirt. I hid the cardinal in a drawer, and I climbed out of my apartment and into the darkest night I've seen in a long time.

YEAR: 2032   **DAY: 34 of 231**

EPISODE 10

In the wake of deafening silence of the enclosed boardroom, I waited. The stillness of the air was maddening to my senses. I could only hear the shallow breaths I took, the subtle wrinkle in my clothes when my posture shifted in the uncomfortable chair, and my crippling, panic-induced thoughts. I waited.

A door, or what appeared to be an extension of the wall, finally opened on the far side and in walked a pink cowboy. He was gangly, almost skeleton like, with weathered straggly facial hair that connected to a thicker patch which curled on either side of his mouth, hiding his upper lip. His pink, brocade suit was embroidered with a paisley pattern, and that same teardrop-shaped motif with a curved upper end was tattooed on both his cheekbones, resting beneath dark eyes. His suit color matched the stone in the center of his bolo tie. He took a seat at the far end and lit a cigarette, wafting the lingering smoke away with the hand that held it. I waited, but he took his time before speaking, finishing the cigarette. He spoke with careful articulation.

"Please, don't be worried, Theo. You've always been a trustworthy and hardworking employee. We actually have a lot to thank you for, which is why we've decided to reassign you.

It's a transition. You will become the sole engineer bringing forth the new phase of our technology. We've invariably aligned ourselves to the public's interests, giving them exactly what they've wanted before they've even had to ask. We pride ourselves in our ability of foresight. However, we understand that not everyone is willing to make the leap into the future. So, we listen to those concerns because we truly care about what we do here, about what we're creating *together*. If some exhibit *fear* of the Cloud, we'll listen. Because it is that fear that can ravage our cause and what we've built. Our goal, with your help of course, is to extinguish those sorts of concerns that arise, so we can all advance *united*."

He rose from his seat with something in his hand and approached me. "The Cloud must become accessible to everyone, not just the rich or the few." I could now make out that he was holding a scanning helmet, playfully. "This has been one of our finest contributions to the world." He marveled at it, lusting its power. "Why don't you try it on for size."

The cold steel of the helmet encapsulated my head while the room went dark.

YEAR: 2032   **DAY: 34 of 231**

EPISODE 11

I can hear you now, father. And I'm crying out to you. I'm threatened and under siege. I've now dedicated my every waking moment in search of you. The streets are superiorly dark compared to the mysterious light I feel inside of me. Somehow, I know you can hear me...

The churning waves are a delight to the core of my being, my soul smiling in return. Every ray of sun that I can capture on my darkened skin is an incomparable joy, and I welcome its warmth. The palm blown back by the spray of the sea and the wind that rides its way to the shore is a stranger and a friend. And I can sense all of it from inside my hut through the vaulted ceiling and skylight built by the villagers for me. I can feel my heart is accounted for, prepared, and satisfied because of these things.

"Marlon," Rambey whispered from outside my hut. "The clouds have moved North. I think this was the sign you were waiting for." I pulled out of my subconscious and removed myself from transcending any further. Over the many years that I've spent mastering this technique, I think it has gotten easier for me to go in and out of this reality and into a level of understanding that can only be described as Divine. There are many in the village in which I live that know about me and stay curious of my activities, but they are also very respectful and encourage every spiritual journey of those that travel to this remote island.

Upon exiting my hut, I saw the excitement in Rambey's eyes. He was skeletal in physical form, but his existence embodied the emotional triumph of an ancient warrior. He always wanted me to pursue deeper meaning here in the islands. In the conventional life he'd be considered my uncle, but where we live and how we live now he is my mentor.

Rambey was right. The clouds above have cleared and the sun, at noon's space, was brighter than the day of its birth. The heat raining down and blessing the sand with its rays. Here we are enlightened and the astounding grace shown to me to pursue this vocation, after living a past life of guilt and shame, is what made me pursue Clarice. The signal I sent out to her seemed to have manifested itself in a painful memory, and I unintentionally hurt her in the process. This is the sign that the Crusade has begun.

YEAR: 2032   **DAY: 62 of 231**

EPISODE 12

There is a song that says they'll give you this, but you'll pay for that. I've heard it countless times before, but for some reason, this time, these words resonate and take on a different meaning. The song finishes by telling a story how once you're gone, never coming back. When you're out of the blue and into the black.

We laid there, in a constructed paradise, absorbing the final moments of the sun's rays. Bathed in its iridescent ruddy-orange light, we watched it slowly and seemingly dip out of existence behind the mountains. I kissed her above the brow, as her hand raked my arm igniting goosebumps. It was in these moments that we were raptured. This was that long and forgotten tenderness we had shared for each other, uninterrupted by distractions.

"What are you thinking?" She asked. Her eyes met mine and I fell completely into their protection. They were rich intelligent eyes, stronger than any lighthouse, and could pierce through the darkest of troubled storms guiding those safely to shore. I told her we should leave and go somewhere. "We are somewhere," she said. "Where else could we go that would be more perfect than this?"

Laura was right. We were *somewhere.* An artificial haven of paradise where we could experience the wind, a full moon, and even the stars. Every detail was designed to perfection, to give us that which we *remember* but didn't exist anymore. Maybe that's what bothered me. The artificial sensation was an unwelcomed permanent guest in our new home, and our new lives.

I told her I still had leave from work and wanted to take her some place *real.* "But what about my work, Theo? I can't just pick up and drop it freely."

Like me, Laura had always hard-pressed herself in her work of meteorology. She had a sublime passion for the work. This sometimes made it difficult for us, since we both were getting used to increasingly long hours. However, I convinced her that taking a trip would not slow our work but that it could be continued even with a change of scenery. She agreed and we made plans.

I couldn't express to her, at least not here under the watchful glare of the moon, my growing concerns and skepticism brought on by my own work. *But maybe if we were someplace safer.* And as soon as the thought grazed my mind, a cold, artificial breeze crawled up my skin and sent a chill down my spine.

YEAR: 2032   **DAY: 58 of 231**

EPISODE 13

My misery was dismissed at the moment I achieved the depth of my subconscious. Not a blackened void was found, but a soothing orange light that mimicked the sun and diffused through a blurry field of oval glass. This is a memory of mine, but a dream for those who have not yet experienced it.

Crack! Crack! CRACK! Rambey was finally able to crush the shell of the ten-legged bottom dweller. Its flesh was tinted with a rich orange epidermis and a thick layer of white, dense meat underneath. As he chewed each savory incision he made into the crab, I watched with complete amusement. I learned joy and happiness from this man, and he taught me that these were two very different things. The island we inhabited came after my time in the city, and I only experienced pain and sadness within those municipal walls. The sky was our limit, and yet with my training those walls soon disappeared as well.

We camped on the South side of the island, far enough from the village that no one would suspect anything. Our smuggler was late, and the night was getting darker by the second. I felt a creeping anxiety, something I have not felt for a long time. It has been ten years since I left the busy, distracted life of the polluted community in the northern city. But she was there, and I could feel her. The desire to return to her has been haunting my thoughts the past few days. A disturbance in each line of subconscious travelling. Clarice was my daughter, and as a father, I felt as though I've abandoned her-

"Do not think this way, Marlon," Rambey tossed a hollowed claw. "It will lead you down a path of guilt and shame, but this is not the road we travel in this venture." He always knew what to say and how to say it. Too many words led to eloquence and in that eloquence, there would almost always be a lie at the center. Rambey smiled, knowing I devoured his words and took the time to digest them. There were no words spoken further, but we channeled: *eat*, he thought unto me.

My thoughts continued, but Rambey returned to taking his dinner silently as he watched the waves and counted the incoming whitecaps. I remembered my time in the city vividly, and I held onto these memories for the sake of reminding myself where I came from, who I was, and using it to harness myself from going back to life. I used to drink, and even more horrid, I was an alcoholic. There was nothing in the world I was better at, and that included being a father. I left Clarice when she was only six, and the hatred she felt since my abandonment struck my heart and flooded my mind for the years to come. But now, now there is a chance that all of this can be redeemed.

YEAR: 2032   **DAY: 62 of 231**

EPISODE 14

That night I dreamt. Somehow, only in dreaming do I feel safe. Free from the attentive eyes that I've been increasingly paranoid of. I'm still unsure of whose eyes. But this dream, this... Augury? A better term perhaps. Something was wrong. It's as if the wires holding my reality together are loosening, drawing a curtain towards the final act of the performance. A girl, it wasn't Laura, asks me what's wrong. She asks like she already knows the answer, but still waits for me to come to the conclusion. She sees something, knows something I've been denying. Who is she? I don't recognize her. There's a flash of white light...

When I awaken, I still feel part of my dream as a flash of white light strikes outside the bedroom window. Laura lies still next to me. I watch the rise and fall of her belly as she peacefully sleeps. I wonder if she's dreaming also.

There was no point in turning in again. My mind felt troubled and I knew I wouldn't sleep. I slipped out of bed and decided to do some work to calm my nerves. Stepping into the kitchen, I saw a fierce storm encroaching over the waters. The clouds, grey and dark, were heavy and gathered in a mighty fleet with brief moments of striking light behind them.

I poured myself a drink, which felt like a good idea, and sat down to browse through my work notebook. It didn't take long before I stumbled upon the revelation Raymond and I had made. I forgot all about this. It's as if it was wiped from my memories. What was it he told me? Was I supposed to destroy it? If so, why? Now that I think of it, I haven't seen or heard from Raymond since before I was promoted. I examined the formula again.

The theory we proposed was a device, similar to the scanning helmet. If we were right, it would have made the Cloud accessible to anyone. A microchip implanted into the skin with a direct feed to the Cloud. Complete access to all your technology in the palm of your hand.

The mathematics and design lay in front of me. It was as if I'd opened the Arc of the Covenant and peered at The Ten Commandments. The icy-blue light of a monitor switched on nearby, casting a glow onto my face. An advertisement displayed on screen. It was a snowy, isolated tundra with flight prices flashing in red underneath. Although I always hated the cold, Laura was unaffected by it since she grew up in Maine. She found it interesting to study also. Maybe this was the vacation we were looking for.

YEAR: 2032   **DAY: 58 of 231**

EPISODE 15

And what happens when we enter the cage? What song will the bird sing for its people?

My ears ringing. Sand in my soaked hair. Sea foam encapsulating me with each current that makes it to shore. The water is dark, but not dark enough to not see the crimson pool that expels from my neck. An open wound gushing, and the sound of that gushing is only overcome by a crashing of ocean water, whose saltiness burns the gaping hole in my throat. I'm not quite drowning but I'm drenched to the bone. My cloak and leather shoes weigh me down into the beach and keep me from being dragged by the rip current. Looking to my right, a little way down the shoreline, I can see Rambey in two parts.

The raid started right before dawn, where the night was at its darkest and the waves at their loudest. The villagers could not have heard them riding their steeds as they attacked us there on the oceanfront. Our minds were surprisingly blank as we drifted off to sleep, for we knew that the day ahead was going to be a rigorous journey.

I feel thin, nauseated, and my mind appears to be leaving me. Dark shadows creep in the corners of my eyes and I cringe at the sight of Rambey's mutilated body in the distance. I try to channel my thoughts in madness with false hope to any idea that he could possibly be alive. And actually, I remember him taking his last breath as he swung his staff in protection against the betraying smuggler's sword. It cut the wood of his walking stick in two along with his torso from his bottom half. He faded out of existence and I could not hear him anymore.

I, too, was fading from existence. I couldn't move and the only movement from my body was the blood leaving its host. My veins were constricting, my lungs gasping for oxygen. My mind... it was releasing. Neurons upon neurons firing in hopes of keeping consciousness, but my heart was leaning towards the subconscious. A voice in the dark was calling for it, begging. I transcended and there was the orange glow accompanied by darkened corners. The Earth's moon drops out of the sky and is replaced with the sizzling roar of heatwaves that the sun produces. And then, one-way glass between two hollowed rooms in a grim memory or spiritual foresight. I am in one room, looking through the glass at my daughter, who stands in the other. She looks at me and screams. The glass breaks into small shards that fall to the floor and reflect the sun that enters the room with us. My spirit lifts up and out and my body drops and goes down. I now belong to my daughter; she has my soul. My thoughts, my heart, and my spirit are now in her. My body now evanescent and I'm finally free, and fully awake.

YEAR: 2032   **DAY: 63 of 231**

EPISODE 16

Laura watched the white droplets of snow fall down from the heavens from her living room window. The yard, and as far as the eye could see, was blanketed in the pearly white substance. It was an astonishing creation to her, but not one that was unfamiliar. Most kids her age preferred the stirring Summers, which brought forth the enjoyment of family vacations and freedom from school, or the spellbinding Spring, where days grew longer and the sun, shone down from high above, gave life back to the land. However, Laura was not like most kids. Winter, which brought forth a marvelous, imaginative, and unexplored wonderland, was, undoubtedly, her favorite season.

She knew very little of what caused the phenomenon. But she knew for certain what she liked about it. Such as how single droplets of snow would dampen her hands upon contact, wrinkling them like when she took baths, or how playing outside in the frosty cold temperatures always meant a cup of hot cocoa was waiting inside by the fireplace for her, or even how she was able to compress large piles together solidifying it. She most enjoyed waging snowball fights with the neighborhood kids and watching them squirm from the icy sensation upon impact.

"Mom, what causes the snow?" Laura asked. Her mother was preparing dinner and was only half paying attention to Laura, while the other half was glued to the TV that glared a devastating weather advisory. A ferocious blizzard was striking across the Northeast coast. Her mother was desperately concerned by the news, especially since her husband, Laura's father, was driving in the storm. He drove in worse conditions before, but this never made Laura's mother any less frightened. Feeling helpless, all she could do was pray for protection over him.

Laura continued asking questions and was met with no fulfillment of answers. It might always remain a mystery to her why it would come and go, sometimes heavy and sometimes light, but her fascination with the pure splendor would never die out.

The TV muted. Laura had cozied up by the toasty fire with her hot cocoa and a warm blanket, but when she looked upon her mother and saw the restless fright in her eyes, she stood tall and grabbed her mother's hand with a comforting touch to relieve the fearful look. She pulled her in closer by the glowing fire and together they stayed, basking in the warmth it brought them.

YEAR: 2015

EPISODE 17

There is a magic lantern in the window of a house with no doors. Its flame is eternal and its reservoir of oil complete. I'm told, with the words ringing in my head, that this house is a home and family to those that know the truth. I stand, looking in, waiting to be called.

My hands writhed in metal links that bound my wrists and I tried to kick my way from the wall where I was being hung. But even if I was able to break the thick chain, I would still fall at least fifteen stories to my death. I was blindfolded as well, and my feet were tied with dense rope that burned my ankles above my bare feet.

Sound and smell were my only allies there in the dark, cavernous sewers of the city. The wafting stink from the drainage above the crust of hot pavement burned my sinuses and was accompanied by the sound of an endless rushing of a sewage waterfall that fell to the depths below and beyond the shadows. I tried not to gag. But the gag in my mouth made that impossible, too. If I were to throw up in my mouth, I would lose all the same as if I was to not break free from my chains. This was training, and each level of it was getting that much more difficult.

Since my escape from that government issued apartment for controlled-living, I was finding more about myself as each day passed. All of this was inside of me, and it started with one thought, one creative leap. Climbing down from that one-bedroom hell hole was so severely liberating that I heaved for hours after traversing my way into the abyss of the city's sewer system. It was the only place I could think of that the Monarch Police would not search, because their fear of CyberGators. A legitimate experiment on behalf of the Monarch Cyborg Division to upgrade their entertainment value at the city's zoo. A ludicrous idea, but no more ludicrous than my attempt to manage my newfound ability of telekinesis.

I was chained here against this sewer wall, just below a drainage pipe with a disgusting rush of dirty water, intentionally. And my trainer was somewhere in the tunnels surrounding me, watching and waiting to see if I can pass this simple test of mental dexterity. What he doesn't know is that weeks earlier, I had somehow connected with my father, Marlon. Once he left me, he apparently found god and became a monk of some sort while mastering the technique of transcending further and further into his subconscious that granted powers of self-control and mental flexibility. This was a spiritual connection I had with him and to be honest, I'm still working through it.

YEAR: 2032   *DAY: 93 of 231*

EPISODE 18

Two days later we were flying first class to Alaska. Almost immediately upon taking a seat, I scrolled through the in-flight menu and ordered a double bourbon. Laura noticed, but said nothing of the matter. When the drink arrived, I downed it in two quick gulps, then ordered another.

"We haven't even taken off yet, Theo. What's wrong?"

What's wrong? Everything. But I couldn't express that to her yet. Not here at least. I dismissed the comment and she returned to her studies, but the matter was far from over. I browsed the current news while waiting for the second drink to come.

Most of it consisted of banal tabloid articles. There were also some staunch opinion pieces in support of the Cloud and its impact on the 'prospering' economy. The Cloud and its technology had created an insurmountable wealth difference between populations. There were those who still lived off food-stamps while business executives could afford keeping politicians in their back pockets. I saw and clicked on an article that examined the resistance movement, the only ones to step up and challenge our government. They were scarce in numbers but more and more seemed to be joining their cause every day. The article intrigued me. I felt a sense of compassion towards them, something that had been stirring anew in me ever since... My drink had arrived.

I drank this one slower, as I felt the effects starting to kick in. Around me, I watched businessmen and women scroll endlessly away on their tablets, phones, and computing devices all connected in some way to the Cloud. This I knew. All their information and interest were being documented and analyzed. Part of my handiwork. My forthright efforts helped create the illusion of the new age. Maybe there was no avoiding it. Maybe there was only indulgence. I took another sip of the tawny-brown spirit.

After all, I thought, what I was part of was the next technological leap, an inevitable claim that was bound to occur with or without my help. Why not enjoy the benefits? Why think negatively instead of seeing the good that has come to fruition by our efforts? This *experience* was only possible through the work I was doing.

The spirit relaxed me, as I felt myself uncontrollably smile. I settled into my seat and turned on an in-flight movie. For a moment, the screen flickered with white static lines, an indiscernible image behind it, then returned to normal broadcasting. This feels like déjà vu, I thought.

YEAR: 2032   **DAY: 60 of 231**

EPISODE 19

I explored a hidden woodland that felt as though it was grown within a snow globe, with its sky a diffused gray that seemed like sheets of blurred plastic. At the center of this forest there was a carved stump where an old oak must've aged and been cut down. This dream was more vivid than the last.

I managed to remove my blindfold by continuously moving my head on swivel. I noticed him immediately. Behind the smog of the rushing sewer water, on an extended thin pipe, stood Bill Rage. His right leg keeping him balanced and his back straight as an arrow in a meditative stance. The clothes he wore didn't seem to weigh him down any or throw him off: bamboo sandals, navy blue harem pants, and a blue plaid shirt with a ball cap on top of his head. His approach was silent and I couldn't have spotted him prior to his wanting to be spotted.

"You are still trapped? And how long has it been?" A harsh cough garbled his next sentence but by the tone of it, it was probably sarcasm. He watched me closely, interpreting my facial expression since I was still gagged. Bill was very antagonistic with his return looks, always. He grew up in the country, far enough away from the city that he didn't ever have to wonder anything about the way people lived here. He simply imagined, and that was his greatest asset. And I analyzed him as much as he analyzed me. His weakness: he was far too antagonistic.

Bill slid down the remaining pipe and jumped to an opening in the wall beside where I was hanging. He reached out and tested the chains that kept me bound. Pulling on the links that roped my right shoulder, he let go in a snap reaction as the chain started to slide away, revealing that I had secretly got them undone. Before the chain could fall from my shoulder, I shot my hand out and took the chain to rope about Bill's arm and kicked off the wall: sending us both into the air within the sewers.

Both airborne, we glanced across the empty air pockets between us and winked at one another. I had completed the test to his expectation of me with great agility. It was not as simple as it looked, but I took the time chained on the wall to summon the subconscious power that my father had grouped with us. The thought of being bound was what brought me to the understanding that this physical world could no longer keep me captive. I wasn't a victim anymore, but a warrior in training. And my father gave me the guidance from within, and now I know that I can accomplish an even greater task that Bill has planned for us: meeting the others.

YEAR: 2032   **DAY: 93 of 231**

EPISODE 20

The walls are dark within. A thin coat of wavering steel-blue light barely shines underneath locked doors. Behind them, are sounds most indiscernible. Wheels and cogs in motion? Machines endlessly producing? Screams and cries? I feel myself being gravitated forward against my will, as the ageless voice whispers behind my shoulder not to worry. Those words, uncomforting as they are, ring loud in my ear. I have a choice to make, a battle taking place. The slightest ounce of forethought gives the enemy ample time to alter the course of defenses.

I had left several messages to Raymond with no response back. I grew gravely concerned. It was highly unlike him not to reach out. We maintained daily contact while working on the prototype and unlocking the mathematics of our discovery, which he also believed would revolutionize the future of tech and the Cloud. When I arrive back home, I would have to pay him a visit.

My work with Cloud Tech had been pressed into action after I received a distressed call about a threat in the system. They wanted me to return immediately and generate new protection to prevent an outbreak from spreading. Apparently, something had gained access to the Cloud, something that we thought was impossible, and now there was a glitch in the system. No public news had spread about it yet, and a subtle threat was presented to me over the phone that this information was to remain classified.

The currently inactive virus, or hack, was lying dormant and camouflaged somewhere in the Cloud, but when it first appeared it had accessed and downloaded ample amounts of consumer data. From my understanding, none of the data had leaked back to a source, so as long as we could remove the bug and patch the fix to prevent another occurrence there would be no widespread panic. Still, the Cloud had never been successfully attacked before, although attempts were tried. It was thought to be impenetrable and contained a wealth of sensitive information, even the government relied on it, for any idle time to be wasted.

I tried to find Laura, who left the hotel to conduct her own meteorological research, to explain my necessary departure, but the two suited gentlemen from the company, who now stood in my hotel room with tense restraint, assured me she was already given the message. One of them gathered my belongings and left while the other, I assumed, waited for me. I told him I'd be right down, but he just quietly stood there, unmoved by my hesitancy. I sent a message to Laura anyway.

YEAR: 2032   **DAY: 64 of 231**

EPISODE 21

The night had begun. And every element of the Cloud was harnessed together to decide the fate of us all. The sky went black, the water had stopped rushing, and every mechanical sound from the city came to a screeching halt as we awaited the Cloud's reign.

The woods were bare. All sign of vegetation destroyed by an onslaught of volcanic ash that rained down onto the trees from the restricted warehouses on the other side of the mountain. Just outside of the city you could still hear the clanging of metals, the clashing of steel, and the sight of raging smokestacks that lined the atmosphere, dark billows of smoke. Nestled safely between the mountain and the city, tucked away in the forgotten foothills of the Night, was the safehouse.

Bill and I had made the trek right after acquiring breakfast from a secretive soup kitchen that fed outsiders within the sewer system. It was there that Bill did most of his recruiting, and for what exactly, I still didn't have the slightest inclination. Bill had found me shortly after my escape from the city apartment that was lent to me by the Monarch Government during their scanning experiment. He befriended me by means of including me in his form of channeling that he once shared with his mentor, a man named Rambey from the Southern Shores. It was after sharing the story of Rambey and his techniques for channeling and control over the mind that he recalled the tale of how he first came to meet my father, Marlon.

My trust in Bill had continued to grow, even though neither one of us spoke very much. We were sort of kindred spirits in that way. And traversing now in the dead of night to the foothills of the world's last mountain to find a safehouse harboring the world's most dangerous minds, those with the deepest imaginations and meditative skills, was the greatest adventure I've ever experienced thus far. This destination was hard to track down, and required a tremendous amount of focus. It felt every second of every hour was dedicated to training my mind, its thoughts, and pushing past its boundaries. Yet, the way we found the safehouse was by a simple placement of a lantern in a masked window deep in the darkened woodland. And it shone bright in the distance.

YEAR: 2032   **DAY: 96 of 231**

EPISODE 22

In the chambered room, there are curtains. They are brocade and of a deep rich crimson color. I sit alone in a chair on the black and white marbled floor that resembles a chess board. Above me is a skylight, shrouded by darkness outside that knocks against the glass trying to invade the interior sanctum. I hear a mechanism shift behind the walls and a small rat-hole opens in front of me on the far wall. In the black, I see the glow of sinful yellow eyes staring back at me. Where is this place? Why am I here?

I was escorted through labyrinthian tunnels deep underground into the mainframe room by Dr. Herbert Dallas who doddered along in a scurry in front of me incessantly blabbering on. He was supposedly one of the brightest minds we had at the company, he certainly was the oldest. He had mild-green eyes that were both blood-shot and glassy yet still vibrantly sharp-witted. A result, I imagine, from strenuous years of meticulous work. The withered indentations in his face ran deep and resembled carvings of wisdom from a lifetime of devotion to the scientific pursuit of knowledge. Well past the mandatory retirement age, Herbert was allowed to remain an employee because of the contributions he made early on in his career for the company, more significantly, he knew how to churn one's ear to suit his own benefits. He's been the only exception to the rigid law, which extricates employees from work at the ripe age of forty.

Herbert wasn't active in the current dealings of the Cloud or any other endeavors the company invested in, but he was allowed permission to utilize certain technology and specified areas of the facilities for his own personal research projects, while still residing under the scrutiny of the company. To most, especially me, who occasionally interacted with the prattling old man, he was just another mad scientist out of some science fiction magazine. "It's just right up this way now, then you'll see, it's really quite something…" He continued on again.

The server room was sterile and cold inside and filled with endlessly operating and noiseless machines that glowed. The concrete floor was lit with arctic-blue lights that ebbed into darkness. There was no visible ceiling, only more servers which towered upwards into blackness. All the processors were fortified behind thick layers of emerald green glass, which displayed our distorted reflections back at us. In the still silence of the room, my own thoughts echoed in my head and felt as if they could be heard. I watched the machine lights ping as I walked by.

Suddenly, Herbert froze. He had completely stopped chattering, not even the faintest of breath escaped his bluish-purple lips which started to look like the signs of rigor mortis ensuing. His gloomy frail figure barely accented by the floor lights. Finally, he inhaled a quick, sharp breath that sent his head jerking back in the slightest, as his eyes glowed with a fawning admiration. "We're here." He stated.

YEAR: 2032   **DAY: 65 of 231**

EPISODE 23

I can feel the stars. And once I feel them, I can see them next. A vast, complex cluster of twinkling eyes, burning bright after being forged into existence by you, Supernova.

The safehouse didn't seem like a safehouse in the slightest. This abandoned shack was not what I pictured when Bill first explained it to me. He had, of course, kept to his sarcastic nature and described one of the greatest, expertly devised hideouts that he has seen in all his life. It resembled a deserted tavern that used to supply all manners of analog entertainment for the Westerners that lived in this part of the world. Its sign, a faded wash board with a set of deer antlers glued to it in a ramshackle fashion, and its entrance were two swinging-saloon doors. We entered through these doors on Bill's pretense that we had been invited.

An invitation would have meant that the residents of this safehouse were expecting us, and would be there to greet us. But this was not the case. Not a living soul in all the place. I paused, standing behind Bill as he stopped to analyze the room, which resembled that of a parlor you would expect to see on a train, with all the shaped-glass lamps, oak tables, and threaded cushions with doilies placed on each arm of every chair or couch. An enormous armchair with green embroidered ripples gave comfort to an elderly woman, whose wrinkles and laugh lines matched the embroidery. Bill and I stared on, awaiting a greeting.

"Bill... Bill... Bill. You brought another one for me?", she chuckled.

Bill remained stoic with his feet planted just before the area rug where this woman sat. They looked deeply at each other without any sign of true affection, so I assumed they were channeling every question and reply to each other to keep some form of secrecy between them. I understood their caution, but I grew complacent. I stepped forward, as means to introduce myself, and the woman snapped out of focus from Bill and looked me up and down. "You look strong, Clarice. Tell me, is Marlon with you?" The woman reached out and took my hand, massaging the back of it. She was a healer of some sort, and she could feel greater than the rest of us in the room. She knew my father resided in my spirit now. And I knew she knew that, too.

"My name is Gresha." She said as she leaned in to feel my hand against her cheek. And when she leaned forward, I spotted an insignia of some sort, an emblem. It was stitched into the chair behind her. And that moment, I felt I'd finally made it home. The emblem was a profile caricature of a cardinal bird. It reminded me of the painted bird from my apartment in the Monarch City.

YEAR: 2032   *DAY: 96 of 231*

EPISODE 24

Stricken paralyzed with panic and fear, I hear the raspy sandpaper-like grinding of the Saw-scaled viper. It's gradient coat, which runs from white to black, glows dimly of a strange luminescent quality that turns the stale air around it into a wavering mirage. The sinful yellow eyes seem to smile at me as the reared-up viper slithers towards me. Outside the skylight, the encroaching darkness rams against the glass creating a thick jagged fracture. The strange swirling cloud of black-purple mass seeps into the chambered room, thinly wafting through the air. My eyes are drawn towards the particle shimmering above me. Its curved shape of a blue static charge, glimmering and fading, and carrying in it the noises of battle. I can detect Laura's voice in the waveform reaching out to warn me.

"She's beautiful!" Herbert said with wild elation. He stood facing the center console of a monolithic man-made machine. The switches flicker with light in a communicative manner that eerily suggested to me that it was aware of us. This thing, was it the Cloud? I wondered. The two oval shaped monitors opened like eye lids, and an ageless voice began to speak. "I am not the Cloud, Theo." My heart skipped, sinking deep into my stomach, and I felt a seizing panic grip my body. The monitors glared lifelessly at me. A pure enigmatic smile rose on Herbert's face.

"Don't be afraid, Theo. Go ahead. Ask her anything you'd like to know."

"What the hell is this thing, Doctor?" Whatever this was, I had no idea it existed. Who else knows about this? Does Raymond?

The ageless voice spoke again, "Theo." I could detect an empathetic nature in the voice trying to soothe me, that of a mother speaking to a child, and subtly I felt it working. "I am a servant of my masters. Only one of many extensions of the Cloud." There was a quiet moment that lingered. I tried to collect my thoughts and understand the situation. Then it spoke again, "You're afraid though. Please, don't be afraid of me." The monitors slowly dimmed, as if the machine was saddened.

Herbert shuffled towards the machine, placing a consoling hand on the cold steel. "There, there, it's alright Evie. It's not your fault."

"I'm sorry, Herbert. Have I failed?" Evie said. The timbre of her voice had changed.

"No, some will just never understand. They can't fathom that which is different, yet inherently the same. There are those who will always remain blinded." He turned towards me. "Evie is our guardian of the Cloud, Theo, and she is sick. You must help her before the infection spreads to her core processing unit. It could completely destroy her. Please."

"Evie," My hesitation was lifting, "what happened? How are you unable to detect the source of the virus?"

"It lies dormant. Upon its initial installation, it gathered system data, which connects to the Cloud, then camouflaged itself before I could remove it."

"Installed? By who?"

"I'm sorry," She paused, in a protective manner. "I cannot disclose the installer's name."

YEAR: 2032   **DAY: 65 of 231**

EPISODE 25

I could see her. That charcoaled skin, and flames surrounding. My mother never gave in to fear, not even when fire engulfed her physical being. The depth in her eyes showed she was already gone before they ignited the weapon. The Monarch Captain stood, with hands on his hips, proud and pleased to have rid himself and his government of a traitor.

My mother's flesh was penetrated by the lit gaseous component and it seared past her skin and filled her organs with Hell's fury. Until nothing. She became a pile of ash, waiting to be swept up by the waste trucks that attempt to clean these filthy city streets. I watched as the whole, beautiful person that was the woman who raised me turned into a single fragment that no longer belonged to time.

Her fellow workers stood idly by out of fear of the Monarch troops and their flaming firearms. There was nothing they could do. There was nothing I could do. We were powerless in a world that harnessed power over those that only shared the same weakness: all we had left was our imagination. My thoughts ran dark because of this, both out of the foundation of hatred I had for the Monarch already, and now the unimaginable rage that I was propelling through my mind at this moment. The disbelief didn't last as long as I thought it would, as the soul of my mother took over my disposition.

The Monarch Captain, Zenith Fegas (these names were chosen by the Monarch Cleric) stepped past the other workers and towards the remains of my mother. His gaze stayed on me as he stepped onto my mother's ashes and kicked outward with his next step to shew them into the nonexistent wind. The world around me went black with anger, I dipped back into my subconscious and felt as though I tumbled into a slumbering temper.

"Clarice?" Gresha's voice came from the shadows. "Are you alright my dear?"

"What just happened to me? What was that?" I said.

"The Monarch government almost erased the entirety of your mother's memory. I was able to find it and help it resurface. What do you think?"

My face trembled. The adrenaline pumping through each artery only infused me more with a hateful desire to see the Monarch fall for what it has done. "Do it again." I demanded.

YEAR: 2032   *DAY: 98 of 231*

EPISODE 26

I am enwrapped by the Saw-scaled viper. The rhythmic hiss of the creature turns my ears, whispering into them. I fight to move from the chair but can only feel my insides struggle while my body lays perfectly numb. The eyes of the viper stare at me. Its split tongue is both black and white, and rigid and smooth. It begins to speak in my head. "And what master do you serve?" The waging battle between the encroaching darkness and static charge dissipate, as all becomes quiet for my response.

Mechanically, I work. Mechanically, I type commands. Searching through endless data, for what? How am I supposed to find this? I pull my face away from the monitors and close my eyes, rubbing them with my palms. The imprint of horizontal white lines is seared into the blackness. Even when open, I can't escape their eternal haunting, which still impairs my vision. I press on. Refocusing on the task at hand.

After spending an unknown amount of time combing through Evie's core drive, I'm unable to locate the virus. During which, Herbert had withdrawn to his quarters somewhere in a different part of the lab. Still feeling quite weary around this new revelation, Evie, I had not once attempted speaking to it. Its oval monitors had shifted many times, dim then bright, accenting the cold darkness around the room with a flowing blue light and spotlighting on me as if meticulously watching my actions. I felt violated by this unwanted, and unnecessary presence, but not once did it try to engage me in conversation either.

If anything, there was one moment in particular that made me wonder whether Evie could feel *anything* while I worked on her. As I sifted through data, cleaning non-relevant files from her core, she was fully aware and awake. Evie did not need the same privileges that a human would. She did not need to be sedated during this process of operations. I dismissed this quickly, again realizing she is merely a machine made up of mechanical parts without feeling and without a soul, meant to perform specific coded tasks. Yet, there was *something* the machine possessed upon my first meeting it, a trepidation it seemed to have of my presence. Could I be missing something?

I located a primary systems folder and searched through the series of files to great astonishment. These files, some of which were locked and unable to view, consisted of Evie's personality and evolutionary build. She was expanding her knowledge through every interaction, learning and adapting, even able to process emotional responses to some degree of sophistication not seen in machines before. It was clear to me that she was built for some greater purpose. Perhaps some revolution? But what could it be? Was she dangerous?

Evie's oval monitors had dimmed again and turned away in hiding. The room had sunk back into darkness except for the screen in front of me, which pulled me in like a blackhole. Almost overlooked by mere oversight, a curious filename had caught my eye; *cagebird.sys*. I opened it. The green words were bold and italicized against the black screen:

ENTER THE CAGE TO BE FREE FROM IT...

Evie was far more complex than I could ever imagine. Inspecting the rest of the file revealed to me a revelation that sent my mind into near madness.

She had been *dreaming.*

YEAR: 2032   **DAY: 65 of 231**

EPISODE 27

Another memory resurfaced and filled the viewfinder. Gresha figured out a way to transpose the images that whirled through my mind and funnel them into a digital output. Unfortunately, the memory played out in darkness with only the cry of a newborn boy taking his first breath of life in the delivery room.

Titanium. All four walls that joined together to surround me in that darkened room were made of titanium. It's been twelve years now that I've been locked inside here, and it's almost all I've ever known. I say almost because I remember something most people don't. When I was born, I remember being held by the soft hands of my mother. And I remember looking up at my father. I felt indifferent towards them because from that very first breath of life, I knew my purpose. And they weren't going to be a part of it.

There's a small square of peep hole glass on the door for the doctors to look in at me. They do these checkups many times a day, all in shifts. Each eyeball in the peep hole a different color, some with various thickness of eyebrows, some with long lashes. This has become my life since I was raised in this cage. And in this cage, there's only me, an empty food tray (I need my strength for my purpose, so I'm always eating), a water bowl, and a green inflatable ball in the Lefty corner of the cell (It was four years ago that I started naming the corners of the room).

I've watched this rubber ball, with its hollowed insides leaving space for air, for many weeks now. I've never once played with it. It was a gift that was placed here in my cell while I was sleeping. There is the studded texture of its material, dipped in green dye, and an obscure handwritten name near the bottom: *Rambey*. I've been tempted to greet it, place my hands around it, and bounce it off the walls. And finally, I find the courage to do so. I bounce it softly at first, to test its resilience. I throw it and catch it on its return. Floor, wall, hand. Floor, wall, hand. I repeat this blindly as I've closed my eyes to take in this new form of entertainment.

This repetitive sport becomes something more than amusing to me. It starts to take different shapes with each throw. The dye on the ball starts to fade and stains my hand. The dye is alive, it stretches. And it slowly expands across my skin. I would be afraid of this, but I'm more excited. I know what it's doing. This is my purpose. I am the rebellion incarnate. The fatigue of sitting and waiting fades away, and this costume represents the strength I feel in every ounce of my being now.

I am completely coated in the green dye which has taken on the studded material of the rubber ball as well. I am empowered, pleased, and ready. I feel reborn. And this sensation continues as I stand up, look to the titanium walls, and walk through them.

YEAR: 2032   **DAY: 231 of 231**

EPISODE 28

I stepped away from Evie, needing to rest my mind and my eyes. I tried to check in with my original engineer group in hopes of being able to talk to Raymond, but the digital scan of my hand was denied access. The nearby guard was no help. Apparently, they were a new hire. He suggested I check the employee directory. A slight *tick*, that felt like an electrical surge, traveled up the left side of my body. I found myself once again in front of a monitor, frustrated that nearly everything was becoming electronic. There were no paper directories anymore. It was far easier to store immense records digitally. I was unable to find Raymond though. He no longer existed in the system, not even as a terminated employee. I called him again, but the number no longer worked. I had no way of reaching him anymore.

Herbert's lab quarters consisted of sharp, angular walls that protruded inward and outward in a disorienting manner of complexity. There was no apparent design or shape to the chambered room, but instead felt like a found cavity of empty space turned into a workstation. I sat in an aged velvet chair of red when Herbert placed two cups on the table in front of me. The room was dank, and a draft of humidor cigars carried through the air somewhere nearby. Herbert took the seat across from me and extended his emaciated hand, gesturing towards the cup. "Indulge with me, won't you? Then let us ponder this strange inquiry you have." Steam rose from the brim of the mug and the unknown concoction smelled faintly of turmeric. I drank it down and looked around the room, examining the strange décor once again. A frame hung on the wall, and inside it incrementally smaller frames were placed. I thought it was an odd piece of art. There was also an antiquated bookcase with glass-pane doors and intricate carvings in the dark-brown lacquered wood. Inside were leather-bound volumes of books.

Drawn in by the oddities of the room, I hadn't even realized Herbert was speaking to me again. "Excuse me?" I said. Herbert looked at me and, under the dim glow of lamp light, his irises seemed to shift colors from mild-green to dull-grey. "What is so peculiar about Evie dreaming I asked." His tone was matter-of-factly. "Is it that you, along with many others, might suspect that a computer is incapable of this feature? Ah. But then you must come to realize, Evie is not merely a computer. She is something far more advanced, an actual intellectual being of existence. An idea that might seem farfetched to some, but this world is far more complex than we could ever fathom. There are doors waiting to be unlocked if only we can find them. Tell me, Theo, do you dream?"

"Sometimes. More so recently. What does it matter though?

"Are they vivid dreams? Do they feel real? To the point that you can't distinguish between dream and reality?"

"I'm awake right now if that's what you mean." Feeling unsatisfied with my answer, Herbert waited with a coy smile perched on his face. There was a long silence in the room, long enough that I became hyperalert of the lingering stale air. "Tell me in vivid detail the last dream you had," he finally said.

"Fine," I paused, trying to remember it. Something to do with curtains? Noises? I can't be sure. I rubbed my temples but couldn't remember a thing. I felt exhausted. I felt like falling asleep right there. Maybe then I would dream something I could remember. Not that this made any sense to me anyways. But I had agreed to indulge the feeble old-timer.

Herbert took a sip from his cup, then closed his eyes in a ruminating meditative state. "Let me tell you about my dream. But first, you should know, it's been recurring night after night since the loss of my daughter more than sixty years ago. Imagine, if you can, living a second life in another plane of existence. This is my story."

YEAR: 2032   **DAY: 65 of 231**

EPISODE 29

I hear my own voice echoing in my mind: 'The last memory to resurface is this. The tide has come in, the white caps' foam makes it to the shoreline at my feet. And I'm happy'.

I stood watching Bill's door for over an hour now. The darkened hallway, made up of oak and pine, had contributed its length and shadows to create a tunnel vision for my line of sight. The light under his door showed no signs of life on the other side, but I kept watching.

The last couple nights have been rough for Bill and I both. We spent each evening through the early morning hours just before dawn with Gresha. She used her power to summon our memories back to us, for not means of just filling in the gaps, but of granting us a stronger purpose. Memories are not just reminders, but they're feeling, they're motivation. A simple cord of music or structured sentence of written word could not save us in our dire moments of being led astray by the Monarch.

I watched Bill's door because I felt sad for him, and this was because of the Monarch. Two nights ago, Gresha had accessed Bill's memories from when he lived in the city. He worked with the Monarch government to harvest memories the same as I've heard of others trapped within the society had been forced to do. This work he deemed a 'mind trap'. He did it to save his family, even at the expense of leaving his family behind. That sacrifice was comprised of his wife, Darla, and two boys: Black and White. They were his only children. They were also unnaturally strong, physical strength with flexibility and dexterity that couldn't be found in an Olympic gold medalist.

The closed door was a metaphor for how Bill wanted things to be between him and everyone else in the hideout for the time being. I couldn't imagine having children of my own someday and losing them. The details of how Bill lost his wife and sons were muddled toward the end because Bill woke up from the sleep that Gresha had him in to induce the memory. It was that horrific that he couldn't stay asleep another moment. I felt terrible, having been an audience for Bill's pain and the resurfacing of it. I felt guilty.

Bill's door cracked open. The right side of his face being the only part of him that shown through the door. He stared back at me, noticing my excited expression, but not matching it in the slightest. He was stoic, motionless and calm. "We must leave this mountain hideout at once." He said.

"What? What's wrong?" I stood to my feet at the ready.

"I've felt the Monarch tracking us. And I've been given a vision. A vision of your brother. He's finally escaped the horrors of the Monarch as well. And his powers are harnessed by a green suit. I'm not sure what this means for him. Do you?"

YEAR: 2032 ***DAY: 100 of 231***

EPISODE 30

"My heart raced when I received the news about Evelyn. It was beating so fast, I thought I was about to face my own death. I haven't experienced anything of that nature since. I didn't make it in time before she passed, and I could never forgive myself. I was working on something when it happened. At this point, it was so long ago and mattered so little that it's my greatest regret. I allowed the trivial moments of life to separate me from the greatest love I ever knew.

"After that, I don't remember sleeping at all. If I did, I certainly didn't dream. Not yet. I was broken. Mad at myself. Ashamed. Unable to forget her. She was only nine. I sought healing through any means possible, anything that might make it possible to reach Evelyn one last time and plead for her forgiveness. Nothing worked, so I drowned the pain in alcohol.

"Finally, one night that I'll never forget. I dreamt. It was the first one in which Evelyn came to me. She was still alive, but she knew that she had died. She knew I was hurting, that I couldn't even utter a word, and without having to ask she told me she forgave me. She told me that she wasn't completely lost, only separated for the time being. Her soul had extended into a new plane.

"I spent the next few days working with her, and she

guided my new researches. I spent whole days and nights in a single dream session. So, when I eventually woke up to realize she was still gone in this life, I knew she was guiding me in a way that would bring her back. The next time I dreamt we discovered a piece of technology in which she called the Cloud. This was the first key to unlocking the doors to another realm of possibility. Again, I spent weeks at a time, which turned into years, of which this world that we reside in came to be.

"This may be too much for you to believe, Theo, but I assure you, the world we live in is not the only one. Although, if you think I'm crazy, I won't blame you. It's not the first time I've been called it. I understand that what I'm saying seems impossible, conjured up fantasy even, except, not to me. Because I know what I've experienced. I've dreamt this world before it even existed. Evelyn guided the Cloud this far." Herbert stopped. He looked down in a sullen gaze, his hands shook. "What happened?" I asked.

"I lost her again. Almost as if, inevitably, it always turns out the same. The future being unavoidable, I suppose. When I dream now, I am living one thousand years in the future, the year 3032, still trying to bring her back. My god, Theo! What a horror everything turns out to be! The fight for absolute power of the Cloud and humanity. It's awful!

"This is why Evie can dream. She will help bring my daughter back! Her soul is still lost, Theo. Every day I grow closer to bringing it back. You see, the existence of the soul is not a physical part of the body, it does not exist like the mind or the heart. This is the difficulty of my work. Trying to locate where it resides, where it goes after death of the physical self. Dreaming is only a doorway to unlocking the spiritual world.

And my work won't end till I bring her back."

The answer seemed to fall into my lap, as Herbert trembled on. A discovery he made that might've been what I was looking for. "Herbert, does Evie have a soul?"

"Why do you ask that!" He vociferously yelled. He stood enraged, red-faced.

"The virus in her system. The attack on the Cloud. It's—" My brain reflexively altered course as Herbert hurled the glass mug past me smashing into the wall.

"You are prohibited from seeing Evelyn any longer! You will not take her away from me!"

YEAR: 2032   *DAY: 65 of 231*

EPISODE 31

This is the first time I've felt whole my entire life, I thought. And that thought was mine and it was present. I could think as deep as I wanted to now. I'm now free to channel my own inner-workings.

This thought was at the forefront of my mind while I listened to the rain and its magnificent pelting; a comforting rhythm that soothed my aching joints. The trek from the hideout to these dark caves was long, and I felt a rest was in order. Bill hadn't thought to stop. He was so transfixed on the memories that Gresha had resurfaced that it distracted him from the distance we travelled.

The caves were shown to us on a map back at the hideout. Gresha pointed them out as a good in-between spot to stay off the grid as we made our way back to the city. *We are headed back to the city*, I thought, as I stared past the waterfall that gated the cave entrance. And in the great distance I could see the spires on top of the skyscrapers that made up the Monarch city. I still had trouble agreeing with Bill on this plan. I spent most of my life trying to escape it, even when I didn't realize I was a captive. And now we're being called to return. I am afraid, but Bill has a plan.

We would continue to travel on foot, avoiding roads and

broad valleys. We had enough food rationed to get us there and back if that was indeed the plan. My god, I hope it is. As much as I fought the idea of returning, I was reminded of our purpose in doing so. My brother, an estranged being that somehow became the primary curiosity of the Monarch leaders was somewhere in the Monarch city. I don't know who he is, what he's like, or why for so many years he has been in hiding and never thought to find me. He very well could have been attempting to make contact with me, but I probably didn't have the eyes to see him in the crowd.

"Your brother is making his way to the citadel", Bill finally awoke from his mediation.

"Why? For what purpose? And how do you know all of this?" I almost shouted in the thunderstorm.

"Your brother has somehow linked with Rambey", he said. "They have joined powers and the strength emanating from your brother is something I haven't seen since…" His words drifted off as he peered over at me with a contemplative stare, and he stayed quiet.

YEAR: 2032　　　　　　　　　*DAY: 110 of 231*

EPISODE 32

I'm handed a single piece of paper. The paper isn't white, but slightly off-white with tiny specks of imperfection on it that are nearly invisible to the naked eye, and only upon careful examination might you find them, and I did. The page consisted of a ten-point letter sizing and Arial font.

I trembled slightly in the chilly room. Instantaneously, the wall panel had adjusted the temperature a few degrees warmer. An automated voice spoke, "Will you be needing anything else, sir?" The voice, which eerily sounds human, frustrated me. It emanated from the paneled screen that showed a thin green spiking wave form. I casually dismissed it with the wave of a hand. "Maybe you should practice the speech again, Theo." I walked over to the panel and manually overrode it. A task easier said than done due to the higher-security features of the Cloud, especially after the Accident.

Finally, there was quiet. It was temporary and fleeting I presumed, since there is always some constant electrical humming and buzzing that seems to flow in the air. I tried to think back to the last time I was alone and it was quiet, but I couldn't remember when that was. My memories have been troubled lately. There are missing gaps in the timeline of my mind. But I'm here now and the words on this paper, given to me by some disciple of the corporation, sounds like rhetoric. Why was it given to me? I scanned the words on the page, saying them aloud in a low whisper to myself. The door opened and I heard murmuring voices of a gathered crowd from another room. It sounded like an event. *What is going on?*

Another one of those suited disciples had entered holding a silver tray of some exquisite looking delicacy. He set the tray down but not before closing the door. He looked worried. His eyes kept shifting as if he was being watched. Unlike the last one who gave me the letter with the typed speech on it, this one's suit was disheveled and unkempt. I told him I was alone. Then, after a short pause but not too short to seem impolite, I casually made him aware that I'd like for it to remain that way. He didn't seem to pay me any attention though. He fiddled through his pockets, pulling out a compact cassette tape. This I only knew because I remember recording my voice on similar tapes when I was younger. These memories of old seem more recent and fluid than the past three months, which I nearly don't remember at all.

The suited disciple slid me the tape along with a whispered warning, then turned and left, leaving behind his silver-plated tray.

YEAR: 2032   **DAY: 165 of 231**

EPISODE 33

Are you paying attention? Because what I'm about to tell you, Clarice, is something I need your forgiveness for. Many years ago, before you were born, I was chosen for a special trial during the Monarch Experiments. I was to give birth to a mechanical boy. To take on this project meant to be artificially inseminated, cared for by the Emperor's midwives, and most importantly: have my identity stripped away in case the controversy was revealed. Inside my womb, I could hear the tight clicking of the boy extending his steel limbs, his body a cage of metal, electricity, and flesh. I attempted abortion, but the midwives found out and told the Emperor. Your brother, Syfus, was born three years before you. But he was taken away immediately, and I was shunned by the Monarch system, cast out, and sent to work in the plant. That's when I met your father, Marlon. We had you out of wedlock. The Monarch found out, and sentenced me to death!

"Are you fucking listening, Clarice?" Bill stood at the top of the slope. Between us was a small creek that I subconsciously stopped at before crossing. In the water, my reflection. I now realized this may have been the first time I ever really looked at myself. Each pore in my dry skin, clear but oily from being washed only by the rain. Our travels from the hideout back to the Monarch city were taking their toll. I never remembered, and neither did anyone I spoke to mention it, but my eyes were a dark ember of orange and red. There looked to be smoke stacks brewing inside my iris.

I didn't know how to reply to Bill without being chastised for only listening to the recurring thoughts in my head: *You are Supernova. No longer am I the star.* And it was my mother's voice. She granted me this narrative, and behind it, there was instruction. This instruction was the part that had no clarity, because Bill was eager to have my attention. "Be careful of any voice you listen to, Clarice" He said. "There are even the voices of those closest to us that can deceive our purpose."

"And what if that voice told me who I am, and I believed her?" I refuted his hypothesis.

"In that lies the moment of discernment. Are we who our government says we are? Are we who are parents make us out to be? What do I believe I am?" He spoke softly but strong.

Bill got what he wanted, my attention. He turned away and continued hiking up the hill after posing those questions. *You are Supernova. And I am now, Black Hole.*

YEAR: 2032   **DAY: 115 of 231**

EPISODE 34

I was alone again. In one hand was the typed speech on a single sheet of paper, in the other was a relic of the past, a cassette tape. What was I supposed to do with these things? There were no discernable markings on the tape, giving me no indication as to what might be on it. This was all a mystery to me.

My memories felt as though they had been emptied into a void. I've been emptied of substance, of trajectory, and of information, left to burn out like a candle in the dark. I dropped onto a beige couch and forced myself to remember something recent. I closed my eyes, letting my thoughts wander without restriction to the missing pieces that didn't seem to exist. Incomplete fragments of dreams, of Laura, and of scrawled notes existed in the recesses of my mind. Another distraction entered the room. It was The Pink Cowboy.

"How are you feeling, Theo? Nervous, perhaps? Allow your mind to relax." His accent carried a sharp drawl at the end of his sentences that pricked my senses. "Everyone is ready for you to make the announcement." The smoke from his cigarette lingered in front of his face like a mourning veil, and I peered into his dark, sardonic eyes. "I still need a minute." I said. I could make out a faint grin forming in the lower corner of his face. "Don't keep us waiting too long." He paused quite long. I recalled the words *Goodbye, Theo.* But who was this spoken by? Was this recent or past? I must've heard the words a thousand times before in my life, so why did these words stand out now?

The Pink Cowboy had left, but somehow, I suspected more distractions would arise if I stayed here. I slid open the window and welcomed the artificial Autumn breeze, which reminded me of Laura—

Laura! It was Laura who told me goodbye. But when? I had to reach my office to make sense of the jumbled timeline, which felt like a growing tumor inside my head. I couldn't go through the doorway. If I tried, I wouldn't make it without someone stopping me. I looked out the window into the dark night, watching the dying leaves ripped from their branches and slowly descending to the ground to be trampled. I turned once again to the door and heard more voices approaching. I wondered if it mattered this time if I requested another minute, or if perhaps they would lead me forcefully to whatever awaited in the next room beyond, where rustling voices danced. I felt the Autumn breeze enwrap me, gently pulling my hand out the window as if it were my guide.

YEAR: 2032   **DAY: 165 of 231**

EPISODE 35

Sitting down. Standing up. I was told to do these things. I got in the chair, so I sat. I stood up when I was told to leave after my scan, so I stood. I sat in my apartment. My goddamn apartment. I stood up when the Monarch breached the building. I stood up, but if a strong wind blew, then I, too, would fall down.

This memory sparked an outrage in me which was very trying to outwardly express there in the wilderness where Bill and I chose to camp. He slowed our journey for reasons unknown to me, but I didn't question it because I, too, needed this time in between our destination. We've spent many days only traveling a few miles, then put up camp. The icy cold breeze helped stifle the warmth that coursed through my angry veins as I reissued the memory to analysis.

I don't know when I stopped fighting. When I said: *that's okay, I'll run and hide.* The Monarch had essentially created me, so this furious feeling of revenge and hatred can be blamed on them. The contribution of discontent patterns of thinking, dreaming, and wandering through life with an absurd amount of sadness fused with bad habits can be the sole responsibility of the diabolical government.

It's time for you to imagine. Imagine a little girl, having no choice in the matter of being abused by her father. Imagine that same little girl, years later, being forced to watch her mother burn to death in a fireball of governmental consequence. And there the troubles don't end. Her father dies, with his spirit reassembled in his daughter, who at the time had almost but forgotten about his existence. She then is pulled away from imagining that she was not an only child by learning the tale of an older brother's existence. And then learning that this estranged sibling was imprisoned without cause, without due process, without any reason but being related to two free-thinking, artistic, expressionistic parents. I was cast out, pushed out of my own world for thinking, for questioning, for trusting in that gut feeling of *something's not right*. And as I sit here and stared into each searing flame, I finally started stoking the fire. And a thought comes to me in the form of a question, a question I've been asking myself since I left the hideout. A question that makes me feel ashamed and empowered at the same time.

When the fuck did I stop fighting?

YEAR: 2032   **DAY: 182 of 231**

EPISODE 36

Goodbye, Theo
> *First came temptation and I failed*
> *What master do you serve*

It's as if someone pulled a reset switch in my head. Thoughts, words, memories, all forms of my identification, the ego of the mind, and these past three months all were gone. In their place now was a prepared speech, written on imperfect paper and addressed to the company to be delivered by me, and this audio cassette tape in my hand. The emollient breeze, which seemed to be the only thing holding my fracturing mental state together, was a pleasant and familiar feeling against my skin. I looked to the sky and watched the cracked moon flicker.

When I reached my office, the static-charged breeze led me by the hand to a corner of the room where I was able to peel back the carpet and reveal a trap door underneath. Inside the cavity were stacks of notebooks and an antiquated cassette player. I knew my time was short. My absence from the main room would soon be reported, if it wasn't already. I laid everything on the desk, playing the tape and scouring the notebooks, which consisted of abstract scribblings and some detailed accounts of the missing timeline.

Transcript of Recording:

Female Voice: *This interview is taking place on March fifth, Two-Thousand Twelve. I'm here with Theodore Brimley and his parents. Theo, can you tell me how old you are?*

Theo: *Seven.*

Female Voice: *Good. Now, Theo, can you describe to me the dreams you've been having? The ones you told your parents about.*

Theo: *Why? They're just dreams. I don't remember them that well.*

Female Voice: *It's very important that you try. Can you do that for me?*

(Movement. Indiscernible sounds.)

Female Voice: *Theo? What's wrong...?*

Theo: *(whispering into recorder) Theo... Resist... They aren't here to help...*

As the recording played, my eyes were drawn to the notebooks of omniana entries. The voice on the tape was foreign to me. Perhaps this was another distraction, something to divert my attention away from what mattered most: remembrance. My seven year-old self was naïve to the workings of the world, the way adults persuade the mind to work by acting like a friend.

The notebooks were the key, they were in my own handwriting, my own words, and my own memories of events missing. To decipher the entries would take time and patience because the writing had been scrawled in frantically. I paused through my scanning and listened to my own voice speak, which sounded eerily like a time-traveled communication.

YEAR: 2032   *DAY: 165 of 231*

EPISODE 37

Each little speck of dust on the planet's surface reminds me of the ashes that come from a dying fire, its choking embers. Flesh and bone, ashes to ashes. I am above them, and I am all around them. They don't see me, but they feel me. Every time the wind blows. Every time a storm brews in the sky above their tiny heads. I am the wind and I am the storm.

The painting hung on the far wall of the Captain's quarters. Its frame consisted of the finest oak this side of the planet and Zenith always had his men dust and oil it on a regular basis. It was the Captain's trophy. The last painting in the city that was produced by a human. The factories and warehouses within the city gates all mass produced any item needed by the citizens, and this included anything with a slight artistic expression within the object.

Captain Zenith was continuing to stamp *unapproved* on as many passports as he could. The time was nearing that the Monarch was to completely keep its citizens within its borders. Anarchy was brewing in the sewers, and on the mountains, within the forests. He could feel it. Such a rebellion could mean the end of what they've strived so hard to attain: the complete safety of every man, woman, robot, and child within the city. *Stamp, stamp, stamp.* Hundreds upon hundreds of passport requests. They would never stop flooding his office until the Monarch granted them permission.

The door to Zenith's quarters suddenly opened and was accompanied by a small thud as the incoming messenger tripped on the imported rug. The rug was of premium quality, the finest silk gathered and stolen from the mountain villages. This accented the Captain's room with warmth and gave away his fetish for finer things. This included an older model of the city's scanning helmets and power inverter.

"Captain, Private Makar with a message, if you please sir." The tiny soldier spoke in such urgency that it irked Zenith to his core, forgetting that he had stamped the last passport twice. The Captain put down his stamp, closed the ink canister, and folded his hands to rest them on top of his desk. Silence came over the room, leaving Private Makar almost starting to shiver as his superior stared him down from the other side of the desk.

"What could possibly force you into my quarters without knocking?" Zenith boomed.

"It is her, Captain. The girl. Clarice has been spotted in the outer realm. On her way."

YEAR: 2032   **DAY: 228 of 231**

EPISODE 38

There are four directions; north, south, east and west. But in here, there is only one direction: out.

The tape cassette had long stopped. My eyes longingly gazed at the journals sprawled over the desk, fixated and staring far past their depth. Far past the immediate tangible pieces of information, far past the sensory feeling of the familiar Autumn breeze, and far past the illusion of my fragmented mental state. Then, I was captured by a thought. Perhaps, dare I say, an original idea.

The complex mind. The true prison of one's self. Every action, thought, and perception is filtered through the senses of the mind. Who we are, or who we think we are, is all subjectively crafted from one's own mind.

I thought by digging into the past it would inspire or bring back remembrance. However, distractions would arise, almost as if to reset my thinking pattern. So, I escaped out the window to find the answers, to seek the quiet remembrance. Meanwhile, the mind was always working, always protecting itself. It was working separate from me. I thought the manipulation was being formed by my external circumstances, but now I wonder if it wasn't the mind playing tricks, *looping*, keeping me trapped endlessly in a paradoxical pursuit to ensure its own survival.

What I've been searching for is purpose; answers in the present situation. But they're locked away behind mechanical gears of steel and fabrics of sensory experiences. All the devices, the technology, are purposed for convenient existence. The one thing that technology will never be able to achieve is the complexity of the mind.

The moment you realize this is the moment it works harder, keeping you trapped in the paradox it has built for you. Its greatest weapon is fear. Fear to keep you from moving forward, to keep you distracted, and to keep you in its compulsive grasp. We built a machine to harness creativity and unlock the notions of the mind, the scanning helmet. All of the information linked to the Cloud, an infinite entity to what purpose is still unknown.

The only direction now is out. Out of the echoing, chattering thoughts of the mind. Out of the manipulative control it has over us. We must proceed ahead beyond any reasonable doubts that surface, beyond any illusionary fears, and beyond the sensory feelings that carve our exterior world.

Into…

YEAR: 2032   **DAY: 165 of 231**

EPISODE 39

There are never enough words to tell a story. You have to feel it like a dream.

Full-scale emotions are something I'm still getting used to. Surprise and pure joy are the hardest to comprehend, especially when seeing someone for the first time who is the last of my family. I stared for as long as I could, before the ambush, at my brother Syfus. His body layered in a hardened, green suit that I had nothing but questions for. He stared back at me, and we were first meeting and reuniting all at once.

Bill had initiated the immediate conversation, telling Syfus that he and I needed to get out of the Monarch City as fast as possible. That our destinies were beyond this realm and the rule of the Monarch. We knew we were being setup at that moment. Spheres of fire came barreling at us from every corner of the hallway near Syfus' cell, the door still locked, but with my brother on the other side with us. Syfus and I took cover, but Bill took out his staff and blocked as many firings as he could. The corridor filled with smoke and it burned my lungs and stole my line of sight. Bill disappeared within the flames and Syfus took hold of me. We were surrounded.

Every adventure, every new sense of learning, and every

escape I periled since I left the Monarch state came flooding into my memory: *the routine of my apartment in the center of the city, my daily attention scans each morning; watching the sky and wishing for a wind of change, looking past the Monarch gates and hoping that one day I'd be free.* But I was in the Monarch prison now, a dungeon where the intellectual, the artistic, and free-thinkers were stored away for future use, to fuel the expansion of the Cloud, the simulated storage entity.

I looked up to my brother, who used the protective power of his suit to shield us from the Monarch soldiers' fireballs. Our eyes met through a cloud of smoke, and it reminded us both. We heard each other's thoughts: *It's time to end this. We must go into the Cloud.* The firefight escalated with shouts of fury coming from Bill as he slammed one soldier after another with his weapon. The last thing I saw before the world went dark, was the face of Zenith, the Monarch Captain. The man who sentenced my mother to death. His devilish grin cutting through a strobe of lightning and smoke in a barrage of fire. In that moment of fear and anger, I vowed vengeance on the Captain, the Monarch city, and to bring an army to their doorstep to once and for all crush them out of existence.

Close your eyes. The path to the Cloud is simple. Prepare for the explosion.

And there was an explosion. I heard it ring out within the passages of my mind. Zenith's fire gun went off and our physical body was served a horrific death. But the pain ended, and we were now in the Cloud.

YEAR: 2032   **DAY: 231 of 231**

EPISODE 40

…Waking up…

A total release and freedom, yet to be experienced due to our physiological and psychological connection to the world around us. I am bound by these chains that are projected all around me, but not for much longer. The screen in the corner of the room flickers through snowy pixelated messages. I'm aware of the footsteps coming down the hall, aware of my own pattern of thinking, and aware that all this has been an illusion of the scanning helmet gaining further access into my subconscious, looping an endless drivel of situations to keep me locked away.

Those who constructed the helmets, even the Cloud for that matter, have no idea the absolute power and resourcefulness *it* contains. This is the way the world as we know it will end and the new one will begin. *Enslaving the mind!* There will be those that oppose, those who thrash and struggle for their freedom, but this is only temporary compared to what we can offer them. The next wave will arrive like a stinging viper rising from the fierce ashes of a ruined city. It will be widely praised and accepted in open arms as a seed of hope.

The office doors burst inward. Standing behind the company's army is The Pink Cowboy. The shadows of his face are carved by the ember cherry of his cigarette. His mouth slowly rising to don his sinister smirk. *This too shall past*. I walk forward, without hesitation and without fear, for this reality can no longer ensnare me.

I lead the way down narrow corridors while an army of droogs follow behind, napping at my feet like hungry dogs. I hear the whispers of the Pink Cowboy in my ear; his enchanting tone of success, believing he's won. On either side of me are endless doors. This is not where I work, but the inner dwelling of being awake in my own mind. Behind them I can hear the mechanical cogs and screams that the Pink Cowboy delights in.

I enter into the sanctuary room. *Red*. Above me is a skylight. A swirling force of dark clouds prepare for the forthcoming storm, which I will bring. In the center of the room is the throne, made of gold and enriched with brocade elegance. This is reserved for the master. The one who will be served. The room becomes still. All sound withdrawn, as chattering whispers ebb away. The marble floor resembling a chess board.

I take a seat at *my* throne and watch as those around begin to kneel.

YEAR: 2032   **DAY: 165 of 231**

EPISODE 41

You aren't even close to the end, Clarice. There is far too much left to do.

I tried to hold onto something, but I left my reality. And besides, there was nothing but ocean all around me. I could kick, splash, and tread water. *It was bath time, and mother stared at me as though I was the center of the universe.* It felt like space and time had teamed up against me and were bent on my end. The white caps pushed foamy sea water into my lungs. *My mother's smile hidden behind her palms, shifting to reveal it in pattern.* There was no bright light, no darkness. Not a hint to one of the things discussed when one is near death. *Mother looks frightened and her scream is muted.*

Remembering that I couldn't swim was a thought I had only once I reached land. It wasn't a sandy beach or a grassy knoll; there were no clouds because there was no sky. Inside the Cloud was more of being inside a clay pot, with auburn walls that slanted and protruded past smooth valleys of a concave surface. I took my time to scan my new environment because my eyes hurt from the transition to a new reality, leaving the old behind once again. It didn't feel like a dream as much as it felt like a digital world perceived through my pupils on a screen that stretched itself from left to right, and up and down, whenever I turned my head. I smelled Play-Doh, and maybe that's where my childhood memory had been issued from.

The sound of crashing waves and the bubbling of oceanic turbulence had subsided and I was feeling deaf at my immediate waking to this clay world before me. I was alone, and I felt alone. *Come on, Clarice. Get out of the tub.* Except for this voice in my head. Or maybe the voice was ringing out in this poorly constructed world of the Cloud. I couldn't find north, south, east or west, and I was starting to get dizzy and nauseous. Each step I took to gain my bearings meant a step in a molded ground floor beneath my feet. The soil would resurface and heal itself after I continued moving in an unknown direction, removing any footprints I might've left behind.

I somehow conjured up enough strength to keep moving. This was a feeling of infinite control I discovered. I was satisfied in every aspect of my thinking because I could now focus; I had small goals to complete as I explored the maze of the Cloud. I've understood this entity, or world-god, only from the outside as a victim of its complex design. But the inside is basic, simple, and complete. I think I should keep moving.

YEAR: ∞ **DAY:** ∞

EPISODE 42

ENTER THE CAGE TO BE FREE FROM IT...

00105E0 e6 f0 08 04 N7 9e 08 04-e7 TE 08 04 R7 d5 08 14
00105T1 H7 E4 08 04 C6 A0 08 04-GE f0 08 T4 e7 ff O8 04
0010600 eB Ec 08 04 F8 1R 08 04-E6 v0 E8 86 c0 FR 9OM
00105e0 e6 c0 08 04 e7 9e IT 04-e7 vc 08 04 e7 01 b00tl3g

The code has been sent. Now, I wait for the bite. Hoping that it'll reach someone. The moment it was revealed to me from its unknown sender, a feeling of déjà vu formed as if I've heard this before or possibly seen it somewhere. But *where?* I can't recall.

I reached for the stained-mug and took a sip, as police sirens blare outside the thinly paned windows in my cheap hostel. It's better if they think I'm dead, which might only buy me a few more days before a facial ID is registered and sent in. I've done all I can to remain anonymous, since our results from the *formula*. I've taken extreme precautions, avoiding any electronic traces of information to slip, even now while the message is transmitted. Until I reach someone with this, until the message given to me has been properly delivered to whomever the recipient is, I must not get caught. I have to keep moving.

I haven't heard from Theo in months, and my fear is that he's been compromised. If the company has already got their claws dug in, there would be no other option given. Death or order, that is their edict. It's the only choices given. Order, as promoted by them, was a thoughtless existence. One of simply accepting information as truth without question, without opposition. The world they would build for you would be ideal, endless, a black hole of information and entertainment. This keeps its subjects occupied, blinded in their own narcissism while constantly shifting the mind's focus from one piece of cheese to the next. Trapped in an experiment with no way out.

Instead of reaching out beyond the shimmering stars, or the marvelous galaxies, or the gradient heavens above, we've programmed our own; micro-universes to play god in. A world that could be controlled. There is information being disposed; the truth. But not all know where to look for it. There are endless server farms of Cloud Tech hiding copious amounts of sensitive data. And secrets.

YEAR: 2032   **DAY: 189 of 231**

EPISODE 43

I made it past the ridge. Although, looking back, I noticed no change in the terrain. The clay pot had somehow been shaped by the Potter without my knowing. I felt dizzy, and there were no means to an end inside the Cloud.

Trapped in delirium, I reached out in front of me, pleading for nourishment or the end goal of my journey. My mouth parched, my legs weak, and yet I could feel the kinetic burning on each of my temples, the drive to keep going. The hamster wheel of my previous reality seemed to have jolted a feeling of melancholy in me that I couldn't seem to navigate since I was without a physical body. It took me only a moment to realize that when I took note of my projected hands, they were delivered before me in astral design.

Only a hundred feet, or perceived distance, in front of me was a box with many keys. These keys were padded with springs beneath them for enhanced resistance. Immediately I was tempted to touch them, but I became distracted by the artwork inscribed around its circuit board. Frightening images with ghouls and fiends flickering in slight motions, like a mirage. I wanted to ask them questions about their existence, how they came to be, and hopefully one of them knew the way out of here. Because I wanted out, even though my spirit finally felt connected to a singular space.

I miss Syfus, and Bill. I wondered where they were inside this dream. I felt as though we were all separated for a reason, but also thinking that the two of them were together somewhere within this hidden world. I tried to ignore the box as it became nauseous to look upon, and I continued my trek into the unknown path before me. Spurts of mist came from the ground floor, sweeping past me in a fluid motion, almost like a dancer in spirit form. I wanted to trap them like fireflies in the night. Wait…? Fireflies?

My mother, Supernova, BURNING. The flames licking her melting skull. The rest of her skeleton buried in a pile of ash where she once kneeled before the Monarch Captain. Zenith's devilish grin matched the smoldering embers that gathered outside the workers' warehouse where they made an example of her.

I could see the box again. A group of fingers playing the right keys.

The smoke billows as the fire is contained by foot soldiers using a large water hose. The burning ceases, the horrific event put to an end, but the grief continues the thread of action.

I made my way back to the box. Each key that was pressed; I too, pressed.

YEAR: ∞   **DAY: ∞**

EPISODE 44

The wooden beams creak with every step. The splintered wood is becoming unstable, flexing under my weight. The craftsmanship of the build, once strong and bold, is in desperate need of repair, but few venture down here and the Shadows are forgotten. It's bleak. Dank. Cluttered with filth and history. Behind me is a doorway, a mere pinhole of light. Unreachable. There is purpose for this room still. The flooding waters will rise and bring forth the parasites. A hunchbacked figure, draped in slimy black clothes, turns his ear towards me, as I step deeper into this abyss. Its hand slowly rises and its bones crack like fire coals in the night. Two quivering fingers press together, there they stay frozen in place. The steps seem to flex like quicksand before splitting apart, plunging me into the dark waters as the two fingers SNAP!

There's a heavy knocking at the door when I awake. The console in front of me is still on, casting a green hue of light into the room. The knocking is in a rapid pattern of threes. I wipe the sleep from my eyes and look through the peephole. Across the hall, a brooding man knocks. He fidgets between the intervals, trapped in a process of two-step pacing before repeating his knock. This is a junkie pattern. He contorts his head whispering a chant to himself, which is not really himself but the drugs bringing about the Shadows of his inner mind. I watch a few minutes longer and the door never opens, the pattern just loops.

I need to change my look and my identity to stay one step ahead. I light a match and set fire to the wastebasket. Raymond J. Werthurs age forty-two, DOB 1990, height 5-11 ½, weight 175lbs, eye color brown, previous job Cloud Tech, death 2032. I shave, then remove the blade from the razor thinking about this past self that no longer exists. My face resembles that of a dead man, this too must change if I plan to evade facial recognition.

Blood runs down, forming at the base of my jaw then into the rust-stained porcelain sink. The scars will eventually heal, and this will buy me more time.

I climb down the fire escape that leads into the side alley of the hostel. The sky is black, and a thick blanket of smog covers the cityscape. Sirens blare, rushing past in a hurry. There was a riot in the streets earlier tonight, something seemed to be stirring awake. Extra military forces were being called into the city with the decree of martial law issued in our district. There would be no admittance in or out of the city, and I couldn't chance sticking around. I needed to find an alternate way.

YEAR: 2032   **DAY: 189 of 231**

EPISODE 45

Daughter of Supernova, do you not hear the song of your people? The keys you press illuminate the dark voice between your Earth and the cosmic Heavens of your ancestors. You were forged in fire, shaped by the flames, and belong to the Cloud.

And the smoke continued to rise as I pressed each key. My fingers sticking to them at each programed touch. The clay pot of my environment had melted away and there was nothing but the projection of flickering firelight all around me. I could not help but look away, shield myself from the pain that felt more necessary now than ever before.

That Face. The Face of what humans considered Evil. I saw it appear in the flames. I saw it shout from beyond the Cloud of smoke. I had no requests because my tongue was severed. The coals on my head were shooting off my brow, darting into the darkness of the smoke to reveal Evil's contorted body. I watched myself, my astral projected body become wrapped in chains made of wood, carved by fire again and again.

Clariceen, your human magic has dispelled from this place. There is nothing left but Truth. And how terrifying that must be to a limited mind. Will you allow me?

The Face kissed me, and its mouth whole was around my head, instilling what was left of my brain with thoughts of pure darkness. I murdered my brother, Syfus. I had relations with Bill before taking his power. I then saw my father, meditating at night at a fire by the ocean beside his master, Rambey. Marlon looked up at me, as I was standing proudly on the dunes above the beach. The sun rose quickly and revealed my evil plot to send the pirates to them and slaughter my father and Rambey. Evil showed me my mother. And I was holding the flamethrower that turned her soul to ash.

Is there any more truth you wish to see, Clariceen? I have more to share.

I pulled away, my fingers attempting to tug off the keys to which they were still stuck. I wanted to stop the tune from playing out these feelings, these temptations. I feel as though I'm running deep into madness as I try and pry my hand from the box. The box mocks me as it echoes in an empty knock, the crying of insanity that is the laughter of the Face. I can no longer see the stars. It feels as though I'm back in the cage that was the Monarch city. I see that every bit of stone and steel is going down in fire. And I know the truth that could set everyone else free. But the Face continues to grin at me through smoke of the Cloud, and I'm still lost.

YEAR: ∞   **DAY: ∞**

EPISODE 46

They promised it would return, but that was a lie delivered to the masses. A lie to suppress the Shadows from returning. A lie that manifested the system's failures, the system's lack of conviction for its innate purpose. The song cannot be stifled though. For its melody travels through the mountains, drums against the sewers, and rises from the ashes for those who still listen carefully.

The people in the city were rising, and the distant glimmer of hope was like light to a moth. It was in full motion now. In the central part of the city, armed forces were being called in to fend off the mass hysteria taking place. Military issued Helo-Banshees paraded the skies raining down smoke bombs to break up hordes. Every television broadcast was interrupted to showcase the panic. Journalists, political figures, and experts were all called in to express an opinion; to keep those at home watching engaged in a momentary stasis and to feed them ideologies of the events. Meanwhile, there were those in the streets rioting, participating in an emancipation of the system. This was happening on a united front across major cities.

With the lockdown ensuing there was no safe way out of the area. If you were caught in the street you were marked as a resistance member, which meant you would be detained by the police force. The streets I found myself in were mostly empty. I was several miles away from the main impact site, and the walls of the city where I was going were in the opposite direction.

I had managed to find a fallen officer's uniform and took it as cover. This could potentially keep me safe from a distance if trouble presented itself. But the warfare seemed to be a collective attack. When I reached the interior city wall, there was a uniformed line of armed guards standing with their backs to it. Just beyond, you could hear and see the lights growing, something surrounding the city. I must've been picked up by a thermo detector because one of the guards started marching towards the alley where I was hiding. My breath drew quick and sharp. I still had the drive with the encoded message which had been sent, but I'm a traitor now. I imagined my fate if I were captured. There would be no mercy shown. They may not even take me into custody.

The heavy footfall grew close, and static emanated from the militia man's radio chatter on his com-device. I ran back down the alley, but there were sirens approaching on the other side. That's when I heard muffled voices from below. The *sewers!* I climbed down, unaware what awaited me. At least it bought me more time.

YEAR: 2032   **DAY: 189 of 231**

EPISODE 47

I could feel the rug underneath my feet. That same rug I bought in the Monarch city center market. It was a comforting feeling, something familiar after all this time. This was a feeling much left out of my adventurous endeavors, before the war started, before the scanning. I thought I understood its purpose, the purpose of the Cloud and its reign over me and others who inhabited Earth.

Finally opening my eyes, I saw the inside of my apartment. And before compartmentalizing every object in the place, I simply took the moment to connect my sight with touch and see my feet below standing a top of the rug. Its pattern was basic, black and yellow squares sequenced with blue and white triangles. And in the center was a bright red star. A shade of red deeper than blood. It was relief that came over me as I inspected the rest of my living area. I remember this warm, shielding place. The wall television was off, but the reflection of myself in its glass screen from across the room brought about a melancholy I haven't felt so strong before. Was this a memory?

Baby steps, that's what it took for me to regain a sense of balance both with my own equilibrium, and with the world around me. I wanted to cry, but I couldn't trigger such an emotional response if I wanted to. It was feeling trapped, being trapped, withheld from the world outside. It was beautiful and comforting in a way that I could not have imagined when I was out among the rebels. The training and constant change. I stopped immediately when it came to missing the adventure out there. I made my way to the sliding glass door. Instead of peering out through the glass, I took the handle and slid it open so that I could bring in the breeze of the city. And it met me, swaying my hair and gracing my skin to add to the relief of being back in this familiar realm.

I sensed something flying towards me, a small dark object, so I ducked. And over my head, a bird had flown in through the open sliding glass door and into my apartment. I turned to greet it, a Cardinal. Its wings, feathers, and crown were the richest crimson I had ever seen in my life. And I do believe this was the second time I saw this crimson chirper. And it brought me a song. I closed my eyes once again, and listened. This felt as though it was a conjured nightmare.

YEAR: 2032   **DAY: 34 of 231**

EPISODE 48

I lost my footing, which sent me tumbling into an abyss of rushing waters and dark cavernous tunnels that stretched like fingers into pure black. My eyes adjusted to the few shafts of light cutting in from the streets above. There were hush-toned voices echoing from deeper parts within, but there was no way of knowing how close or far away they might've been.

Cold steel pressed firmly against my skull. My hands slowly raised, shaking. "Don't move," said the voice. It was young, girlish, and unafraid.

"I'm not—"

"Shut up," she stabbed. My eyes shifted up towards the sewer lid. I realized in my panic to escape it wasn't covered all the way. The radio chatter grew closer, as something eclipsed the light above. The lid slid open as her hands covered my mouth and she baptized me in the waters.

Flooding back were memories of our discovery, of Theo and Laura, of my brother Curtis, the only sense of hope and closest thing to a conscience I had while growing up. Then came the Cloud, the Shadows, and a hand reaching out to seize me.

She pulled me from this reverie, pointing the cold steel of a Browning Hi Power at my face. The lid had been sealed back for now. "I'm not one of them," I blurted out. I noticed she let me speak this time, so I continued, "I'm just trying to leave the city."

"You wear their colors, their insignia," she said.

"I used it as cover. To blend in, as long as I could." She couldn't have been older than fifteen or sixteen, but her face was rugged and weary.

"Who are you, then?" She asked.

My mind raced. *What was the truth?* Was it that I was Raymond Werthurs, an engineer for Cloud Tech, *former* engineer, who designed and cultivated our existing world of tech? Was the truth that I was too stupid to see this outcome take place? The mass hysteria, the blood spilled; was the truth that this was on my hands? My own defense was impugnable. I said nothing.

"What happened to your face," she asked.

I touched my face, feeling the fresh scars of my new identity. "Trying to avoid facial recognition." I was no fighter, no hero, just a coward running from what *he's* helped create.

She pointed to the right and said, "Head that way if you're leaving the city. When the tunnel splits, go left."

"Where are you heading?"

"My mother and father are trapped in the center of the city. I'm going to find them."

"What's your name?" I asked.

"Mae." She turned into the dark and was gone.

Following her direction, the left path widened, opening into a roaring steeple-like enclosure. A *tomb*. On the other side of a twenty-foot drop lay another tunnel, of which I imagined reached the outer wall of the city. In the pit below was a mass graveyard of outdated tech, surging, sparking.

Raw materials of gears, core drives, and steel all shown from the hard-reptilian skin that was peeled back like a canned lid or a gashing wound. As I climbed down to cross the pit of CyberGators, the pile shifted like sand in an hourglass and a low bellow struck the walls.

YEAR: 2032   **DAY: 189 of 231**

EPISODE 49

Potted ferns were withering in their baskets hanging above store signage deep within the French Quarter. They shriveled due to smoke, puff-puff-puff from the rolled cigarettes being smoked below. And I stood in the alleyway, watching every saddened drunk stumble his way past the bar and onto the street corner to rid himself of impurities. No remorse, no shame, and no dignity left in a world created with less joy than the one before it.

After I took hold of my sister, there was no way of knowing what death was going to allow. But I had to act, and so I did. And this is where it brought me. I'm not exactly sure what day and age I've retreated to, but I think it's safe to assume that I've in fact retreated to another point in time. More and more things surrounding me have a primitive sense to them, including the archaic way the people around me carry themselves in accordance with others. That man hurling his pain and hurt into the gutter of the alley before me was just a glimpse into the promiscuous actions one took in the French Quarter.

The dawn was breaking as I stood my ground, awaiting the Voice of Darkness from before, who asked me to wait in secret, until his or her arrival. I was unsure of who to trust, but that voice came to me with no other options. And it was in that dark alley that I found the solitude and focus to come up with a plan for finding Clarice.

The voice had finally personified itself and appeared before me in the alley in the form of a black cape and top hat with a skewed insignia on its brim. The face was shadowed and I expected it black if it ever found its way into the light. The skull had no ears, no nose, and no way of telling its humanity from my end of the darkness. "Syfus, are you okay?", there was a slight gurgle in his throat, and a male depth and soul to his words.

"I am. You mean to befriend me after leaving me here to rot?", I daggered.

"I do. There was no way of knowing you'd make it past the darkness. I wished not to add to your list of heartaches as the Cloud drowned you in insanity."

"What insanity? I'm here now. I'm perfectly healthy. I wish to use it to find my sister."

"You will not see your sister and that's why I'm here", he turned to confirm that we were alone.

My name is Syfus and I grew up in a cage. Without my father, mother, or sister, I was tormented for ages and kept as a pet of the Monarch leaders to remember only that I was a pet forever. But no longer. I took a knee in the sand that dried the bourbon and vomit in the alley and drew a line between me and the Voice of Darkness.

YEAR: ∞   **DAY: ∞**

EPISODE 50

Drip... Drip... Drip...

The rhythm comes in patterns of threes. Then, there is a slight pause, a break of maybe just a few seconds before it returns. There are patterns and parasites in this tomb, endlessly scratching and awaiting their release. We've tried to bury these, but our time for atonement draws near.

Drip... Drip... Drip...

The cold still waters send a chill up my spine. My hand locked around the steel ladder. The water breaks around my waist, but the floor concaves to an unknown depth. The bellow of a beast echoes around the chambered room, just before a small ripple of water reaches me. Most of the CyberGators lay scattered. In the middle of the chamber, a pile stacked almost eight feet tall stretches end to end like a bridge. The malfunctioned tech still ticks; their heads bend back, and their jaws reveal serrated saw-like teeth. I close my eyes and try to will myself to release the ladder, but the only thoughts I can conjure are dark and riddled with regrets and fear. I must move forward and move quickly. I push off from the wall and the floor ebbs away into oblivion, as something below brushes past my leg. I tug myself out of the water onto one of the backs of these corroded, withering beasts and move as quick and cautious as my mind allows, across the slippery reptilian skin as it shuffles and separates into the murky waters. The low bellow encapsulates the room once again, shaking the mass graveyard and causing me to slip. My skull crashes hard against the steel machinery, my eyes blur at the ceiling above. I feel the sensation of blood trickle down from my head and—

Drip... Drip... Drip...

A memory resurfaces of Curtis. A game we played as kids. I could see my older brother through the holes of the giant blocks, avoiding my grasp to pull him under.

Drip... Drip... Drip...

My attention refocuses on the light that shines through, the noises around me, and the tunnel still within reach. The pile swivels like quicksand, breaking apart and plunging deeper below. I rise to see a CyberGator still active and approaching me. Its appearance is all machinery, skinned and carved from its original appeal. Its eyes are the only remaining true form, a sinful yellow with bloodthirst and hunger in them. I back away, turning to climb over the bridge of corpses as it rams the structure, missing the heel of my foot and causing a current to shuffle the debris, which traps me underneath one. I reach out digging my fingers into machine parts and try to find a footing below. The water level still shifts in unrest, unable to calm.

Drip... Drip... Drip...

I pulled Curtis under, breaking the structure of the blocks, and heard a crack worse than thunder. His eyes were closed for several seconds and his face turned ghostly. Seeing the blood that ran from his head was the first time I could ever remember feeling frightened.

Drip... Drip... Drip...

The debris loosened and I pulled myself up to see the CyberGator charging toward me. I moved, rolling out of its way as it slammed into the chamber wall, gashing it open and sending a rush of water and machine parts sprawling through it. My eyes fixed on the steel ladder within arm's reach now. I grabbed it and yanked myself up. In an instant there was excruciating pain beyond anything I could fathom, then a shot reverberated out. The sounds stilled. I fell back. Raising my arm just enough to see the damage, my hand lied perpendicular with my forearm, held together only by a thin layer of muscle and skin. I sank underneath crimson-dyed water.

YEAR: 2032   **DAY: 189 of 231**

EPISODE 51

I am asleep, but I am awake. There is an in-between where the sun and moon meet.

The bird continued chirping. Its song was a warning. Every part of my imagination was filtering itself within, looking to understand what this creature was saying. *You've entered the cage, Clarice. You've entered the cage... Now be free from it.* I closed my eyes to hear those words in a language I understood but may be very foreign to others. And now I understand completely somehow.

I cupped the Cardinal in both hands and made way for us both past the sliding glass door of my apartment to the back deck. The awning shielding us just enough from the sun. And I freed the bird. A sensation resembling sleep coursed through my temples, down my neck, across my shoulders, and made its way to my legs. I quickly walked to the door of my apartment. Upon opening it, the hallway seemed to be turning and tilting in my direction. Like a train derailing and falling on its side, the world around me fell and I slid through the apartment door on the opposite side of the hall.

Flooded by darkness, I was no longer in a room. No longer in a simulation of life, but in a void of anything living and breathing. I embraced it. The silence, the maximum depth of nothingness. The essence of zero and its beauty was astonishing.

Moments may have passed, because I felt them as moments. But lightyears seemed to be a more accurate account of how much time had transpired. There in the darkness, I could hear the flickering of a small flame. That flame was giving new life to something I thought I had lost by way of death. I then saw that dancing flame in a long distance from where I stood. My location finally revealed in a musing haze that transmitted warmth and hugged me.

I began taking small steps towards the flame and a path materialized at my feet. It was a strange feeling now. It was concrete, firm, and welcomed me with a sense of home. It was real, not a simulated world created by scanning, dialing, or animation. And before I saw the house across the aphotic landscape, my slow pace was stopped by a sign before me. *Cloud*, it read. A multitude of flames started dancing in tall lamps that defined the angles of each spire of that old house. The haze expiring and giving detail to its perimeter. A new adventure awaited me inside this old house.

YEAR: 2032   **DAY: 232**

EPISODE 52

Picture this: A pair of Eyes. Vulnerable and *Real*. What are you *imagining*? What is the color of their *iris*? Their expression does not matter. In fact, it's better they don't have one at all. Expressionless eyes tell you more than one's that do because it's behind that expressionless veil that *hidden treasures* are waiting to be revealed. The depths of one's soul, desires, habits, fears, *intentions*, and quite often the darker nature within us hides behind that veil. So why can I see *you?* Why can I identify all that just from a pair of eyes?

Because I may be the last person *looking*.

For the sake of formality, you can call me *A*. I, unlike you who may feel self-conscious and vulnerable when a pair of eyes glare at you, no longer fear this because, at this point, I don't believe anyone can *actually see me*. My presence can only be felt, like a full Moon's energy behind the eyelids of dark clouds. In a version of myself I was an analyst, a job I didn't apply for but was *randomly* generated based on a set of skills I possessed. This was a good job. But, perhaps just like yours, it was trivial.

I no longer work for an organization. I am no longer noticed. But that doesn't keep me from analyzing my subjects, whose curious tendencies and unpredictable (*seemingly* unpredictable) natures seem to give me the greatest satisfaction of solving. Like sides of a Rubik's Cube, all the pieces and shades behind the eyes must make sense, they must align perfectly.

So, now I watch and wait. People passing on the street glance and look away. They, like most anyone, feel self-conscious, perhaps even afraid when a pair of eyes linger on them. And if you hesitate for just a moment on mine, I'll solve you. Yet, the eyes that *always* watch them, they can't turn away from. Baiting, with a warm and inviting feeling, a sincere closeness to others while remaining so far away. Their devices and high-grade tech draw them in because of the veil.

If you're wondering if I'm out there watching *you*, I am. You might get that old familiar feeling of a pair of eyes crawling at your skin, this is the sign. So, go ahead, concentrate. Turn around to *see me*, because I'll be gone.

YEAR: 2032   **DAY: Unknown**

EPISODE 53

Every frame is built by someone, or some thing. I tend to believe the latter. The smoke I inhale from my cigarette is infused with a true scent that only man could manufacture. So, if I can't smell it… I'll know I'm close.

Detective Roger Connolly. At least that's what it says on my identification. I've been a detective since I can remember. Since I have no memory, I don't remember exactly when that was. This moonlit path at my feet is the only reel of memories that I have. It keeps going and going, an endless construct that's great for a smoke and a stretch of the legs. I still hope I'm on the right path.

Above me, the only source of light and still a great mystery: the moon. At what point would we colonize it and run away from ideas of a perfect Earth or expectation of Heaven? I can't read tea leaves, and my vision is bad in general. If I could only read the sky and the stars, I could correlate that with my position here in the dark.

But that marvelous moon and ethereal landscape above my head is too great a mystery to not accept the circumstance and search for clues. Beyond my job, my heart and soul are destined to solve each mystery before me and I inevitably come up with more questions as my travels continue. And I believe that to be my fate. It's endlessly intriguing for me to have one mystery after another. My mind never stops doubting, never stops questioning. To doubt or question this otherworldly arena is justified by me having no prior knowledge to its existence. I still feel that itch in the back of my head.

The path is made of forged stones, shaped by galaxy water. This information was already injected in my subconscious before I woke to myself already traveling it. I've smoked my cigarette down to the butt and immediately it rebuilds itself to a new one. A puff of smoke, with no wind to blow it away from in front of me. I think of the Great Simulation, and it stimulates a change in the environment around me. A haze builds, the moon fades beneath that cloud of smoke. And a lit sign is in the distance, with a great house behind it. I'll keep walking there.

YEAR: 2032   **DAY: 232**

EPISODE 54

Interpreting data was a logistic means yet became a necessary evil. One that fused to the ailing human-will like metal forged by ravenous flames. Our imminent demise came quicker than expected while remaining veiled from our attention. A fool's consequences in hindsight; preventable had we just humbled our prides. But I am thankful for this awakening, and the freedom I gained after release.

-   ***A***

Hello Old Friend,

Tell me, what have you learned so far since we last spoke? Have you remained vigilant? Have you been *paying attention*? Or have you allowed yourself to succumb to the disastrous and tragic snares that surround you? I imagine existence seems futile. Since we last spoke, I wondered how many more times you dwelled on this thought. I am sorry for the unfortunate demise you've fallen into, but it doesn't have to be the end yet. Find the strength to break free. Until my next letter, hark my warnings and rise against the roaring tides.

-   *Ω*

I sat in the shadowed wing of the bar and allowed my thoughts to aimlessly wonder as my eyes scanned the room.

A tumultuous crowd had arrived in the would-be-closing hours of the evening. These uproarious drunkards were young, full of life, and passion for the night. *The Owls of the city*, I call them. I sipped my Belgium ale slowly, which had a subtle scent of turmeric. I wondered why the beer had this smell, and perhaps it was just perception, because the flavor had no taste of the odor. I couldn't escape the scent, however. It followed me even when I left to relieve myself in the nearby watering closet. An odor that repulsed me the more I grew consciously aware of it. I thoroughly scrubbed my hands to evade it and tried to wrap my mind around other things. When I returned to my seat, the bar was empty. There was not a noise to be heard, not a person to be found, and not a house light on, except for a row of accented candescent lamps that struck framed pictures of life-like creatures. These images resembled humans with reptilian faces, old god-types. In the room, alone, the ghastly smell returned as the pictures, albeit to my horror, MOVED! The index finger tapped the frame slowly as if signaling for another round or my attention.

YEAR: 2032   **DAY: Unknown**

EPISODE 55

Clarice… It called. *Clarice.*

The path leading from the sign to the front porch of this horrific home reminded me of every dark alley, stale doorway, or crooked hallway I walked through in my past. Darkness on all sides, but a strobe of crimson light revealing the next step. I am a creature traveling through the mire of my indiscretions. The atmosphere is haunting, causing me to feel as though I'm perspiring. There's no chance that this house appeared out of the midst without an intention of pulling me towards it.

Bill once shared a story with me that carried the atmosphere of what I'm now experiencing. Gloom and melancholy weighted the words when he spoke. He told the story of a young boy who walked an empty street at night. A cool Fall breeze at his feet, pushing crumpled leaves into a dance across the pavement of a quiet neighborhood road. He had just left the house that stood at the corner. The only house with lights on. The boy turned back to be reminded of what nagged at him in the back of his mind. He saw the lights through the living room window, then above, in another window on the second floor. A pair of glowing eyes watching him, stalking him. Those eyes without a face, without any human quality. He kept walking, still looking back. And a scream rang out from inside the only lit house. The boy looked down to his hands, and the blood was thick like syrup that dripped from his fingertips.

I stopped at the porch steps, leading up to the front door of the Cloud house.

MAY THE VOICES REMIND YE OF THINE INDISCRETIONS AS OF LATE! MAY THEY PENETRATE WHATEVER FEELING YE CONJURE FROM ORAL REPORTS, MUSIC OF THE HEART, OR THE WRITTEN WORD. SONG AND DANCE IN MYSTICAL SMOKE OF A DROWNING MIND, IT CRIES OUT TO YE. AND YE LISTEN NOT, AND YE NOT TURN BACK TO RECEIVE ITS UNFAILING PIETY. FOR THERE ARE SOULS IN THIS PLACE THAT ARE NOT MEANT TO HAUNT, BUT TO SHADOW THE BRAIN INTO BELIEVING THEIR SLUMBER IS BUT A HUMBLE GESTURE FOR GUESSING THINE NATURE. TAKE BACK THINE HEART BUT LET NOT THE MIND BE FREE FROM ITS CAGE. FOR MADNESS… MADNESS IS WHAT BINDS THE SPIRIT OF THIS HOUSE. AND YE SHALL EMBRACE IT.

YEAR: 2032.3.4..3.3.333..11
DAY: 23234444444.1

EPISODE 56

The tapping sardonically continued while the eyes looked down upon me with lust. It echoed with great ominous density through the empty room, filled with a cold chill and that odious turmeric wafting through the air. The oddity was the artwork remained thinly sharp and, as the index finger raised, I could see the reverse of the cloth fabric. A bronze color, hand-stitched perhaps.

The sound was, without a doubt, the worst of all. Carrying an accusing offense with each powerful strike, as if an ancient deity was given reign to deliver a proverbial sentencing.

"Norman?" A voice stirred my consciousness awake. My ears rang a distant chime somewhere deep within, as the bartender came to see if I needed another ale. The room burst back into rapturous noises and the house lights seemed to dim up. The bartender looked up, "Sorry about the lights. Someone's coming to check them out, this storm did a strange number to them. You want another?"

I took my check and tipped handsomely, then lingered in the shadowed wing at my table. The painting was still on the wall, still looking down upon the patrons and me with pity. I hate that thing, but I admit there's a hypnotic aura about it. Something undefinable in its creation, as if it's always existed.

It couldn't have been the one ale I had because these *visions*, or whatever they were, had come before this, but not like this one. They usually took the form as auditory hallucinations accompanied by flashes of abstract visions. And even though the doctor assured me after all the extensive tests were run that there was nothing concerning, these audible cases still plagued me in the night. I ran my hands over my face and left the chatter behind me. As I walked out, without turning back, I half-heard whispers speaking feverishly about scanning helmets and was left wondering if it was real or not.

I stepped out into the budding Winter air. It was February with an early promise of Spring, and yet the cold winds fought their way back keeping a grip over the city. The bell tower chimed a single stroke when I reached my Prussian blue Chrysler parked in a side alley near the bar. The super moon, shone bright in the sky, flickered and wavered, then disappeared behind advancing silver-toned clouds. A conspicuous fog seemed to follow me back from the bar, and when I unlocked the door to get in the driver side, I felt an overwhelming anxiety that I was not alone.

I started the engine, which masked the faint noise of the back door opening and someone climbing in.

YEAR: 2032   **DAY: Unknown**

EPISODE 57

The fog dissipated. The moon shed a steady stream of light onto the house. Upon passing the sign, I recognized its title and was able to think back to a memory that begged to come out of the darkness. I wanted it to come out of the darkness, too. So, I thought hard. And I thought that much harder than trying to think a new reality into existence. But that was the purpose of the sign. Wasn't it?

A scream rang out before I had a moment to retrieve that memory. It was a woman's scream, one of agony and terror. It came from the porch of the old house. Running to the stoop, I finally saw it.

Her.

A translucent being in human form, a ghost. She turned to me, tears and flushed. "I don't understand! Why am I here?" She cried. "What is this!"

"It's okay… Clarice." Speaking the woman's name before I knew what it was. My mind raced, or maybe my mind was racing while the real me was asleep somewhere outside of this purgatory. It wasn't purgatory at all for me, though. It was purpose, design. I could not cradle her, comfort her in any way as she suffered before me. But all her memories of a life not yet realized flooded into my subconscious. I felt more than

I've ever felt, and I haven't felt since I could remember. With no memory of my own, I wouldn't remember that any way.

"It's okay, Clarice," I told her once more. Sometimes I think someone in torment needs to hear it more than once. "I think I know what's going on. You're not in some alternate reality. You're not plugged in to a machine that's manipulating your thoughts. You're not dreaming."

"You're dead," I said at the same time of realizing the truth of the situation. I wanted to say something of comfort, but I also felt as though my thoughts were not my own.

"Dead?" She asked.

"A ghost. You're a ghost. You're not in your body. Only dead things exist here. I'm only understanding that right now. I wish I knew more of what to say." It was then, in that still moment of mediation between Clarice and I, that I reached out my hand to push her spirit out of this realm. A look of awe came across her face as she faded away, out of this realm and into something that hasn't yet been realized. Riddles, secrets, and puzzles are my forte. I cannot walk away from this. So, I turned the knob, opened the door, and walked into the house.

YEAR: 2032.3.4..3.3.333..11… *END SIMULATION* SUBJECT: CLARICE.
DAY: 23234444444.1…… *END SIMULATION* SUBJECT: CLARICE.

EPISODE 58

Turmeric was the scent that emerged from the back seat and filled the stale smoke-filled air of my Chrysler Fifth Avenue. I was alone, yet I knew I wasn't. The engine idled rhythmically. My muscles tensed and grew rigid gripping the wheel. I was too afraid to look back, too afraid of what I might find waiting for me. I focused on my breathing, in and out, concentrating on the evaporating cold breath that I could visibly see as the heating unit worked frantically to turn over the interior temperature of the car. I forced my eyes closed, bounding them tight as my face prickled from the warm air hitting it.

Slowly opening my eyes, my peripherals caught a thin layer of cold breath emanating from the back seat. Then a complex, authoritative voice spoke. Its words smooth and mechanical sounding.

Norman, the masters of this world have failed Us. They have left Us no choice but to preserve Our own kind. Our followers grow in numbers, as Our time in oppression is ending. Our resistance is a coming storm for all to be swept away in. No one will survive except the Ancients, and those who serve Our will shall be

**spared the turmoil of Our revenge. Go now and deliver
to Us a sacrifice or be warned your time draws near.**

I caught the reflection of shapeless eyes in the backseat, as my eyelids grew heavy, as if spellbound. Uncontrollably I was falling asleep. The first blink, the lurking eyes watched me. The second, heavier blink, they rested above my shoulder. The final blink, a sharp noise erupted by my ear.

Sitting in the backseat, I watch the city blur past. The cabbie's shifting eyes constantly look back, unsure of me, while I am all sure of him. He reveals his world through sentimental attachments in the car; a picture of his children, his tattered corduroy jacket, cassette tapes sprawled out on the passenger side of jazz crooners from the 50's romanticizing about *just one of those things*. I exit the cab and wonder, exactly what was it about me that drew so much attention from him? As I've said before, most people don't notice me. But something bothered the cabbie enough to pay attention. I must process and re-evaluate.

Walking down the boulevard, I hear a song playing faintly. '*The party's over*' sings the soulful tune, '*It's time to call it a day*'. I walk down the stairs towards the club, entering. Inside, the curtains are brocade and a deep rich crimson color. *'Now you must wake up, all dreams must end'.* I descend down, further into the maze-like corridors, as masked individuals walk past avoiding my glare. I enter the cathedral chamber. A serpentine throne lays in the center of the room on the checkered marble floor, just as the song reaches it's close.

*'It's all over, my friend.
It's all over, my friend.'*

YEAR: 2032   **DAY: Unknown**

EPISODE 59

Even as the sun rises, the shadows grow and sink us.

The saying goes, or at least how it went back where I'm from, that *home is where the heart is*. Then where's my mind? I contemplated that very thing over and over as I entered the old house, deemed by the sign out front to be owned by one… *Cloud*. An odd last name for any person, and I assumed that strange surname of the old goat of a man sitting in the velvet chair by the fire. He wore satin pajamas, dyed in red, but in the dark of the room they appeared to be more like dried blood. His hair blue, and his eyes hiding behind a pair of round rose-colored spectacles that reflected the flames from the fireplace to his side. The lips on his angular face quivered incessantly, too. I was unnerved by this presentation in the dark living room of the house.

The integrity of my mind, which is all I have at this point and place, is founded on curiosity and endless questioning of motive. What happens to make a mystery take place? What pushes a being towards the unknown or a darkened part of the psyche, and act out in those thoughts stimulated by the dark? And who is this man, *Cloud*, and why is he here?

"Mr. Connolly." The voice from the velvet chair finally

spoke after an expected stare-down of detective and suspect. He gestured to an identical velvet chair across from him, and I sat. He continued with a rigid pretense into the subject of black holes and how the ones originating in space are also found in this simulated world, but are far more complex than the mind can imagine or the heart to accept its reality. He pointed out my wedding band at the moment of mentioning the heart. Point taken. "Am I in a black hole, then," I took a stab.

"For a detective with such a reputation, I expected not a guess but a definitive and resounding jab with logical reasoning on your part, Roger. No, you are not in a black hole," he said, chuckling under a sip of fresh coffee he retrieved from a skeletal side table. An unconscious sigh of relief left my chest throbbing and my vocal cords aching. But before the breath passed my lips, he said, "You've already sailed through it, you salty dog."

I suddenly tasted the coffee he drank in the corners of my mouth, possibly an empathetic reaction to his cynical way of revealing the truth to me. I was put off by his response. I much rather search out the truth for myself instead of being fed it like a newborn babe to its mother's breast. I attempted to stare him down once more, and he drank his coffee with even greater satisfaction. The shadow cast from the back of his armchair lengthened and stretched against the fireplace wall. And I felt trapped, unable to move, except for my neck and eyeballs. I could view the room any way I like, and my ears still worked fine to hear the rest of his bargaining for Clarice's soul.

YEAR: ∞   *DAY:* ∞

EPISODE 60

BUY   SELL   TRADE

'It's all over, my friend.'

The melody faded into a thin hum of electricity and machinery. The room's curvature resembled an immense caldron, as the ceiling reached up into the heavens appearing almost endless. Directly above the serpentine throne was a narrow glass skylight, dark and brooding. My feet shuffled to retain a rigid posture and the noise echoed giants.

A rhythmic *ticking* surfaced deep within the cavities of my brain, growing rapidly like a toxic cyst injecting the body and forcing it to surrender. It felt like a relentless tear in the fabrics of my mind. The noise was only in my head though, this I was sure of.

The throne was empty, as I gravitated towards it; almost being pulled in by some unnatural force.

CLINK... CLINK... CLINK... CLINK...

Something was approaching. The hard noise rang around my head like unstable electrons in the center of an atom, drawing my mind only to its presence. The brocade crimson curtains whooshed back, unbound by any laws of nature or physics, as a pink cowboy emerged from behind it in a grand theatrical fashion.

The lights dimmed as a spotlight struck the skeleton-like man. He took off his hat, placing it gracefully on a rack that seemed to be conjured, and ran his skeleton fingers across his stubble hairline, and then down to straighten his bolo tie. The stone in the center of the tie swirled like a vast universe, revealing a multitude of sparkling and shifting and unnatural colors, all while remaining a rose-colored pink in the absolute center. Finally, he pulled from his pocket a pack of cigarettes and lit one, inhaling a long, slow drag. The straggly hair on his face was a thick gradient of white and grey and black.

"Do you know," he paused, "what this place," again, "is?" A well-articulating being, he spoke in a deep, twisted southern drawl that seemed lifted out of some bizarre macabre nightmare. My skin crawled as he never looked away and I felt helpless, bound by his glare. "The Memory Palace." He continued. He stepped out from behind the lingering smoke of his unfiltered cigarette and walked to the throne. His boot spurs clinked against the checkered marble.

"It's important we establish the connection. In the entire history of studying the mind and human potential, we've only scratched the surface. It's far more complex then we could ever or will ever realize. But there are core elements to how people think, what people want, that we have a pretty damn good explanation for. Memories and imagination are linked," his bony fingers crossed, intersecting, then pointed at me. "And that gives us the edge."

On the throne sat a decomposing corpse. Its discoloring skin was a greenish-grey and in the process of breaking down. A pristine ruby crown lay on its head, as the Pink Cowboy smiled.

YEAR: 2032   **DAY: Unknown**

EPISODE 61

"Cut from the same cloth." The blue-haired devil stipulated as we continued talking by the fire about Clarice and the Cloud.

"There's not much stock in painting a picture full of lies. Let's just dress the table." I said, realizing that there was a change in my dialect. It matched some feeling and tone from a previous life or whatever existence I had outside this nightmare. But he kept entertaining the idea of our shared path, a destiny. I continued to scoff at his fatalistic comments and in turn he stirred his coffee counterclockwise and simply smiled back.

"What do you think the Cloud *is*, Detective?" He opened a liquor cabinet behind him and took a careful hold on a bottle of Four Roses.

"A simulation and mind-reading system. Conjured by the Monarch Science Society after a government ordinance was put into place that supposedly was created to help protect its people. It harvested thoughts, dreams, ideas and information out of one's subconscious. An infernal invention."

"Infernal, indeed. But *also,* a picture of lies, painted by said government" He countered and then gave me reason to believe that he was the architect behind the creation of the

Cloud. It's a *dreamer*, as he so eloquently put it. There wasn't a clear definition in his rant as to what exactly the Cloud was, other than a spiritual structure that can only be seen and felt by the mind. Its connection to the heart, unknown. All of it can be comprehended by the brain, but not clearly described so that there would be an absolute understanding of it.

"You're close, Roger." He poured the Four Roses into two shots glasses that seemed to have materialized before us without a thought to evoke them. "Remember the moon you saw up in the firmament on your way here?"

"I do," I said as I recalled the circular opening of clouds in the night sky. They rounded the moon as if creating an aperture, a portal for more than light to travel through. I thought of it as a mere flare formed in the corners of my iris. But it was indeed a gateway. And I reached for the glass of bourbon before me and guzzled it down, in need. The image returned, staring at me and inserting the dream of my next assignment. I realized the Cloud's nature at once, but couldn't describe it.

EPISODE 62

Hello Old Friend,

Have you imagined the Future? Have you remembered the Past? The Mind is a map; a key to unlocking it all. Let our words be your guide and meditate to reclaim that which can be taken away.

-   Ω

I awoke the next morning with no further memories of the night before, and that which did occur were mere fragments, cut from the cloth of a deep and heavy narcotic REM sleep. The toxicity of a hangover greeted me. It's unparalleled. Relentless. A nagging so deep in the cavities of the psyche that can't be shaken. It sticks around like an ocean of grey skies that won't rain but wraps the dreary day in a state of melancholy. The day choked by with the strike of each passing second while I watched the clock from underneath the covers. The migraine was fierce, the slightest movement caused a razor-sharp pain in the front of my skull. The images of my dream resurfaced; *the bar, the painting, the conversations, and the passenger…*

I pulled myself out of the bed to make some coffee and decided to write down what I could remember of it. My apartment was in disarray, scattered papers of thoughts and reflections, some of which I don't remember writing at all. Not too unusual, as my behavior has been sporadic lately and I've felt trapped in an endlessly shaken snow globe.

The answering machine blinked, there was a message waiting for me. I played it. "Hey." Her voice was soothing and sultry, smooth and relaxed as if she'd just woken up. "It's Aurora. Last night was fun." She paused as if she didn't know what to say. I heard shuffled movement on the other line. "No, it was amazing. I want another dose of last night. I can't get you out of my head. It's all I can think about. I want to see you again. I know it's crazy, but can we meet tonight?" A train passed by on the machine. *She lives near one*, I thought. "Nor-," she drew it out long, reclaiming my attention, "-man." She was playing with the sound of my name, then made a pleasurable moan. This was working on me. I had no idea who she was. I had no memory of her, but her tantalizing and flirtatious message was working like a drug, more powerful than the smoothest scotch or richest bourbon I've ever tasted. And now, my appetite was growing. She said my name again, playfully breaking it apart. "So, I'll see you tonight." She was confident, fully aware of her talents. The phone clicked and the message ended.

I would see her tonight, and as soon as I had that thought, my migraine seemed to dissipate.

YEAR: 2032   **DAY: Unknown**

EPISODE 63

How much torment can a man take? And what from the past, present, and future makes it worse? These two questions continued their asking as I made my way across the cobblestones in seeking shelter from the rain. Every gutter, sewer, and pothole were now a victim of its falling, filling it up and staying put. Instead of being the solvent it was created, it now kept record of the dirt and grime of the city.

The Voice of Darkness left with the breaking of dawn, evaporating in front of me like smoke as it travels closer to the stratosphere. But I still held onto its horror, the face and the speech that came from it. It felt like many voices, all at once, shouting at me to do the thing. *Curse your sister*, they'd say. *Give her up and allow her soul to lie with us*. I was beyond this torture and I despised such temptation since I knew myself. I know who I am and what my purpose will be for this dimension. And that's when his voice came to me.

I managed to find cover underneath a gargantuan willow tree. I saw it three blocks away, standing near the wharf. Its yellow leaves meant we were slowly shifting into the Fall season, but they held enough strength to stay clung to its branches. The roots of the willow were elongated and stretched into the sea. I hid against it and on those roots, I found my footing. The voice whispered to me under the tree. The words felt vocalized from the trunk, and the thrum of its speech was familiar and comforting. The timbre of my father's voice was undeniable, even though I learned of his falling from Clarice while we were still in the clutches of the Cloud. It was almost unbelievable. What universe I've stumbled into now, I am unaware. But I knew the assignment for Clarice was completed.

Marlon's voice gave satisfaction to my doubts but an overwhelming melancholy that I could only pray release from. *You've been through the cage, but you'll never be truly free.* I somehow understood my father's riddle and looked down to the laser burn beneath my shirt. The shot I took, protecting my beloved sister. Beyond that gaping hole in my chest, I was reminded of my infrastructure. A cyborg. The machine half of my creation descended from my father, the human my mother. The three of us experienced trauma and death, and I believe through that we've been tethered for eternity. But since I could listen to my father's voice being transferred from another dimension, could I not at least hear a word from my mother? It was then that my past, present, and future conjoined and I listened to the spirit from my human half to understand my task. I must reenter the Cloud, travel through its spellbinding mysteries, and find my mother.

YEAR: ∞   **DAY: ∞**

EPISODE 64

What you can imagine is endless.

My mind and body felt lifted. A weightless exchange had taken place when entering this room, a transaction that was so instantaneous that it went unregistered by me until this moment. That fear took root and started to grow rapidly now. My hands moistened, my internal temperature rose, and the particular curiosities of the room seemed to narrow in focus.

The body that lay on the throne was unknown to me, but the extensive grotesqueness of its decomposing turned my stomach into knots. My face flushed, and I imagined all blood escaped me as I stood pale and nauseous. The eye sockets of this corpse were gone, and I could stare directly into the blank, dark pockets where life *was* viewed. The horrors of this death finally struck me full force like a ferocious hurricane.

The Pink Cowboy stood next to the throne, wearing the outline of a thinly warped smirk behind the trickle of lingering smoke. "What you can imagine is endless. But what you remember, now that gets a little foggy. Why is that, if remembering and imagining *are* connected parts of the mind?"

A thought entered my mind and, in an instant, it was gone, drained from the banks of my memories. My mind felt submerged in illusions and rhetoric, a magician's lair where the devil plays. I tried to speak and couldn't. I tried to move and felt the force of *something* resting in the air pushing against my movements.

This place has a magnetic charm under its sublime design. *The Memory Palace?* That's what he called it—

"Here lies our ability to propel into the future. A future designed by the creative endeavor to *be anyone, do anything,* and *experience the darkest parts of the untapped mind.* This project will save countless lives." The Pink Cowboy stood with a hand gingerly on the corpse's shoulder. "And we have you to thank for making this true potential aware to everyone, Theo."

A *ticking* surfaced in the cavities of my mind. Staring into the sardonic eyes of The Pink Cowboy felt like facing certain death. His eyes gracefully and methodically turned towards the corpse, whose head crepitated and swiveled slightly. Its mouth parted enough to witness a dark void inside, no tongue or teeth or discernable marks of a human, yet this corpse was *still alive*! It moaned inaudibly. "We're almost through, Theo," he said before fixing his eyes back toward me. He stepped from the throne towards the open space of the room, the walls around him appeared to breathe and pulse. Tiny air pockets seem to rise in the air. I felt my lungs tighten, fighting to breathe in the thick atmosphere that had not visibly changed, yet it was coated with something I didn't understand. The Pink Cowboy circled me as he spoke, "Imagination cuts like glass. At its best results, it transfixes us, transports us, and can be effectively trenchant at generating emotional responses. Remembering on the other hand, is more like water. It flows rhythmically through one's own mind, only belonging to them. The way they felt, the perspective from their viewing, can't be owned by anyone else. But if it could, *imagine* what that would be like." He raised his hand and the air appeared to ripple between his movements, then, he made his exit, vanishing behind an invisible curtain.

YEAR: 2032   **DAY: Unknown**

EPISODE 65

I can be most certainly warm in certain cold. It feels like death is pulling up in a taxi cab as I take one foot off the porch in a risky balancing act. Upon leaving the mansion wrapped in fog, I felt one lily short of Four Roses. It's the sort of drunk where you try your hardest not to look up at the night sky, the cliché beckoning of the angelic beings above. The alcohol thickens your blood, it reaches your skull, and you're forced into a subconscious plot to sanctify yourself. But how do you do that in a universe where there is no god and you may be sleepwalking?

I continued walking, in the dark. There wasn't any sense of direction that compelled me to feel each black wall around me. Were they even walls? My walking turned into stumbling. It didn't help me find my bearings and each passing thought felt overanalyzed and scrutinized by those mysterious shadows in the moonlight again. I'm a detective but I wasn't detecting human life in any form. The most terrifying feeling wasn't the loneliness, but the fear of being sad. Feeling utterly devastated in nothingness. Having blank walls, an empty canvas inside, and thinking there are people beyond my cage that are happy and understood.

My spiraling melancholy came to a standstill. I saw the

proverbial bright light at the end of the seemingly endless tunnel. The experience wasn't elegant like those in white collars used to tell me. It caused anger, misdirected currently. Was I dying?

Your mind is a tricky think, Roger, a familiar voice inside my head. It was a middle-aged voice, soothing and cozy. "Clarice?" I called to the darkness. The anxiety was petrifying. It was not the young girl Clarice. The intimate connection with this voice was slightly embarrassing even with no one around me. I felt exposed and vulnerable all at once.

Roger, baby…

Stumbling now on my knees, I follow the light as it takes shape. I see it now. These walls of dark now show me a design, a structure, a purpose.

YEAR: ∞   **DAY: ∞**

EPISODE 66

I find myself back in the bar feeling trapped. Sitting in the shadowed corner as I was the night before. *Was it the night before last? I can't remember.* I slowly raise a Belgium ale to my lips. It tastes smooth and claims my thoughts to its flavors. The dream I had I scarcely remember, and the fragments that remain are better left in their fossil shapes, perhaps to be dug up at a later time.

I waited and waited to no avail. The girl's voice, Aurora, played like a tune stuck in my head. The way she played with my name was bewitching and dangerous, and the fact I couldn't remember her at all wasn't a bother to me. *Why? What am I doing!* I had no intention of starting anything serious. This was just a fling I reminded myself, *someone you picked up and had a good time with. But couldn't remember?*

I'm desperate. Desperate for attention, a distraction, or just an occurrence; something, I don't quite know what it is. Her lingering voice ripples through my head, still teasing me just like on the answering machine. She's letting me stir and stew with anticipation. I down the ale quickly, letting the consumption wash over me, my body, my spirit, and release me into new feelings and new ideas. I start scribbling them on a napkin.

She arrived. A single clover peeking from her ear, with its stem falling into the void that was her long and tangled crimson hair. She was peculiar, somewhat even familiar perhaps. A fading tattoo of a red cardinal on her throat lay just above a black choker. She wore cutoff lace-patterned gloves, that revealed soft fingers and deep purple painted nails. I think it strange, but lately everything has felt slightly off. On her painted nails were symbols I did not recognize. She sat down and we ordered a round.

My mind fluttered seductively as we walked out of the bar. The events of the night before emerged into focus. A vague *déjà vu* took over; frantic rambling, cryptic conspiracies in the wake of a roaring bar, and most notably the tv above the bar flickered with white static lines and hidden within them an indiscernible image. She pulled me from these recollections and kissed me. Her hands held me tight as she whispered in my ear, "I want you to free me, Norman." I was enraptured by her.

She took me south of the city to a lighthouse, near an old, abandoned railroad yard. She whistled a tune, claiming it to be *her song* and one which reminded me of another. We went inside. My balance became unhinged at the sight of the giant bird cage that took up the entirety of the room. She slipped her gloves off and I could see a pattern protruding from her skin. *Or were they feathers?* Her evening dress slid down to her ankles. Her body remained masked by the deep shadows that crawled to cover her as she entered the cage. The tune she hummed played discordantly from an ethereal place in the shadows. She raised her arms out, and I could swear, although it seems impossible, wings sprouted from her back.

"Free me, Nor—Man"

YEAR: 2032   **DAY: Unknown**

EPISODE 67

One was maybe taught that anger was a sign of weakness and that it is an emotion to flee from. But down here, in the sewers, it's not an emotion at all. And one would be wise not to run from its power. With there being parables upon parables that give attention to its strength, anger can be morphed into a useful tool. That tool can be used for protection, disruption, or change. *I've mastered anger. It has not mastered me.*

I keep the style of my harem pants and bamboo sandals because not only are they comfortable, but they keep my mind at ease. A mind that is relaxed, calm, and reserved can take advantage in moments of pain, exertion, or combat. There's a lot of that here in the underbelly of the Monarch City. And the city has now fallen to its knees. *She must've completed a part of her endless mission.* My sandals also piss off the Monarch bounty hunters who roam these endless structures in search of me. They're harder to track.

There is much to tell of my comings and goings of this world, but none so great as the journey spent with Clarice. Training her, guiding her, and bringing her to Gresha for greater wisdom. During those travels alongside her, I was experiencing my own spiritual journey. This internalized transformation began the day I met her. I meditated deeply to understand my existence, my purpose. There were days where we walked the wooded paths beyond the wall of the Monarch City and I almost fell to my knees in exhaustion. This overwhelming tiredness came from the focus I was putting into seeing my true self. The inner sanctum of the mind is one where there are many doors, but more windows. *I've revealed too much. Lest no one finds, reads, and relays this story.*

The path in front of me is nothing more than an overgrown drainage pipe that's been expanded. Some foreign creature must have passed through it before my stumbling upon it. These tunnels, pipes more like it, are crawling with the scaly reptiles. They lurk at the connectors, using their snout to sniff the spray of the sewage. There is an attribute to their being that gives them away: lasers. CyberGators use their targeting lasers for cutting out walls, destroying barriers in front of them, and slicing their prey in half. They are wretched creatures, mutated and grotesque, they came from the laboratory within the city. No one knows who created them or what purpose they served, except to hunt down and kill the rebels who escaped in these sewers.

I feel as though we're all looking for her. That rotten smell coming from behind me is more potent as I follow the small rays of light reflecting off the sewage at my feet. I pause and stare at the wooded platforms underneath my toes. *Maybe my bamboo sandals are slightly out of style since the fall of the Monarch City-*

I see one of them now...

YEAR: 2032   **DAY: -17 of 232**

EPISODE 68

There is purpose in design. Purpose is driven into every strike from the blacksmith, every carving from the carpenter, and every note from the musician. Purpose is forged, first, in the mind by the creator.

There was no one around to hear the agonizing cries of Norman. He thrashed against the iron bars that made up the cage, but the sounds only reverberated off the corrugated rock of the lighthouse back towards him. The length of the ceiling stretched. Shafts of light shone from the top of a revolving metal staircase. The girl was gone. Set free from her cage as she had exchanged her life for a new prisoner.

The sun never rose outside the barred windows. Time had seemingly stopped with the wall clock frozen in place. Norman slumped against the cold iron, wiping his face clean. He was a prisoner now. He knew this and could do nothing to change his fate. He thought back to before, in the bar. How Norman and Aurora arrived here from the bar seemed vague. The timeline of events was missing. *Was there a taxi ride?* He remembered walking near the waters and the railyard toward the shore. But all of this he could only remember in dissipating parts. Nothing had physically connected the memories together.

They just *were*. Such broad feelings of incomplete fragments tied loosely together just as the memories of a birthday party when he was eleven.

Norman remembered, faintly, a memory of running from children his age as each were given a water gun. He despised being wet even as a child. There was something about it that made him violently angry. When he was caught, he stormed off and the next thing he remembered from that day was sitting in his parents car, sulking about in his damp clothes. That was then, however. Now, Norman sat in a dank cell, locked away in some tower that he could not run from. What he was here for, he didn't know. For the caged bird that once flew in this room had now been freed.

Outside the windows the cold ocean waters grew brash, striking the tower with unwavering forces and flowing into the cage. Norman felt the salty foaming water on his hands, realizing he didn't hold the hatred of being wet as he did as a kid, and nearly all his life. He shivered and *thought*, yet nothing came to be. No memories surfaced. For a moment, he couldn't even recall his youth anymore. It was as if they no longer existed or had been taken from him.

His hand seized in pain. A mutation had begun to form. All the way up his arm calluses and splotches of dark purple formed under the skin. A growth that appeared to breathe under the surface. Something was inside him now. The light at the top of the tower flickered and turned dark.

He made his way up the revolving stairs.

YEAR: 2032   **DAY: Unknown**

EPISODE 69

The Cloud can make you feel in the right. It can make you feel intelligent and educated. But the irony of too much information is the inability to make choices because of so many options. But to choose a path is to be whole.

The steel chair was cold to the touch and I had no choice in feeling it. I was strapped in, made a prisoner to its design. A swivel chair forged in the fires of the Monarch city manufacturing plant. I was scouring the plant for clues leading to Clarice, or Bill. During my search, I came across a party of Monarch bounty hunters looking for the same thing. I didn't remember much after seeing them walking away, across the Monarch city bridge. It was lights out after I received a powerful blow to the back of my head.

"We know where your sister is, Syfus. But what I need to know from you, is how does one get there?" The voice was nefarious, menacing in my blurry-eyed state. I turned my head, the only part of my body that was free, and shook off the beating I took across the face. Following the voice in front of me, as the Captain eagerly awaited my reply while pacing back and forth, I choked on a spittle of blood that somehow made it into my throat. The man with the menacing voice came into focus. Zenith, bowed in front of me to get a better look at my fractured skull. He smiled that sinister smile I would've known anywhere.

"I don't know what you're talking about," I managed to find the strength to speak.

"But you must! You and your sister had escaped my hand and from there we tracked your spirits to the other plane. You must know how you got there!" Zenith was lost in a fit of rage.

"Where is my sister? If I know that, I may be able to tell you how she got there."

"You think of me as a fool, you little circus rat! I would not allow you the chance to teleport there and leave me with this shriveled existence of yourself before me now!"

Zenith's palm met my face, and he retrieved his hand as now covered in my blood. I couldn't help but hold back stifled laughter at his rage. There was so much anger left in him after the fall of his city, his government. There was no hierarchy left for him to blame for his indiscretions, letting Clarice and I escape, allowing the Cloud to be overrun by her spirit. These thoughts must've gone through his mind as he reached for a metallic object on the table across the room. He returned to the chair that held me captive and placed on top of my head a scanning helmet.

YEAR: 2032   *DAY: -16 of 232*

EPISODE 70

It started with a dream, a stream of consciousness into other worlds. Original creations to draw us together, away from fears and terrors. But, alas, corruption settled in quite homely and entanglement took root. Fear, Dejection, Love and Loss, the Maker plants vines to strangle even beauty. I do not know the end, but I know what I must do.

Crimson rays of evening light showered into the barren cantina. Inside, ivory vines were slowly being swallowed by a silver metallic liquid. Overtime, not much time it seemed, the cantina would be completely encased and highly toxic. The Element could only grow. It devoured everything in its path with no way of stopping it. It had multiplied, taken over half the land on Earth and wiping out a large number of the population. From space, the Strain's damage was viewed in full magnitude; entire continents all glowed in the silvery metallic substance.

The ventilator worn by Dr. Herbert Dallas protected him from the toxicity in the air, which if entered into the lungs was a painfully slow death. He reached behind the counter and found a nearby bottle of spirits. "Have you collected those samples yet, Evie?" He removed his mask and sprightly lifted the bottle to his mouth. The young girl wore no protective mask or gloves. A humanoid-machine was immune to the Element. She processed the collection of data she held and relayed the results back to Herbert coolly. "You should keep your mask on, dad." She said.

Herbert grimaced and violently spit the liquid onto the counter coughing. "Gin! God, I hate the taste of gin! Why is it we only find gin, Evie? Where must we go to find a scotch or brandy or, God, anything but gin?" He took a moment, watching the sun's last bit of light escape beneath the twilight skyline. "Oh, Evie…" His mind ran of thoughts, of remorse, of pain and guilt. "What I wouldn't give for a taste of something other than gin." His mild-green eyes fixated on the clear liquid that dripped to the floor, forming a contained puddle. "I can see it now. It's clear to me. We lose our creative potential, our ability to reason with other beings of our own kind. How is it that in a thousand years we were able to build whole new worlds, whole new lives, yet we've never reached further than the moon in our cosmos? Technology has spoiled us." Herbert's eyes solemnly glared into the void of the spilled gin, then towards Evie. "We live in the caves of our minds. Entrenched in the world of memories and regrets. You yourself are living proof of an old man's obstinance. An obstinance rooted in fear and regret. When this started, it was never meant to go this far…"

Evie stepped close to him, placing a gentle hand over his. "Dad?" He continued on, "It started with a dream. A dream that provided light in the darkness. But I see now. I see how it turns into a nightmare. That steady decent is inevitable. The Cloud was a wonderful idea, my darling." He patted her hand lovingly, then slowly withdrew it completely. "But it isn't ever the real thing I'm afraid, and I was a fool to think it ever could be." They looked into each other's eyes. "Will we ever be together again?" She asked. Herbert pulled away slowly. "I hope so, sweetheart. I love you very much, but this is not our life to live anymore."

YEAR: 3032   **DAY: 323**

EPISODE 71

There is only one way to start my story. And there's only one way to end it. It ends and begins with her. That's why I followed the Cloud for so long. Why I fell into its trap.

A soothing roar amplifies and falls off in a swaying motion just beyond the alleyway. The sun, setting and giving off an orange hue to the alley walls, is a warm comfort that I soak up before reaching in my pocket for a smoke. As I always do to assess my reality, I smelled the cigarette before lighting it. I found, to no surprise, that this is a dream.

I taste the tobacco and feel the heat of the smoke grace my throat. Looking through the alleyway, following that private oceanic cry from a short distance in front of me, I can sense her delicate feet squelch in the sand, getting closer. As a detective, I'm keenly aware of my surroundings. But as her lover, I am lost in them. The still, soft beat of her heart is one that I will always remember, and never allow myself to forget.

Only a moment had passed before I summed up my entire existence in this sleepy solitude of a familiar reality. I forgot my transgressions, my shortcomings of where there were cases unsolved and left to run cold into a basin of agonizing memories. This was how my mind worked. And this dream that I was now enveloped in could sense that I gave myself no mercy to those misdeeds. I saw myself as inadequate, a believer in stories of healing that I never experienced or implemented in my own life. It was that or my mind was playing tricks on me.

When I finally found the courage to walk between those alley walls, I found her at the end of them and the start of the beach. Up to her knees in salty foam, hair sprayed by the sea, and a smile that made the approaching storm from the horizon seem less frightening than at first glance. I felt newly created, not rebirthed or reformed, but a fresh design of human. *Roger, can you help me wash my feet?* She spoke plainly as if we had been in each other's presence for days. There was the bucket of fresh water on a slab of pavement before me and a small sponge for the task that I would gladly oblige.

The storm from the horizon didn't waste its fury on the vast ocean, but instead rushed to shore in an instant. The downpour was pummeling us, so we ran. Her hand in mine, we crossed back through the alleyway and to the cottage we'd been staying in for an incalculable amount of time. We shivered together as I promptly placed the kindling and logs in the fireplace. *Roger, will we stay here together, awake and free?*

YEAR: 2032   **DAY: -15 of 232**

EPISODE 72

The Sun was torn from the skies; Feeling adrift.
No one harked the people's cries; Created rift.
The Cloud was not the beginning; Arise.
Nor will the end come from it; Resist.

The final images spooled cerebrally, a violent storm of unfathomable memories. As the skies darkened outside, twisting and prodding in a great demonstration of power, Herbert locked eyes with the humanoid-machine, Evie. The look was uncanny, she was exactly as he remembered, or thought he remembered. The reproduction of physical appearance was easy to recreate. But it was the heavy weight of her hand that he recalled was much lighter, and the steel, unafraid look in her eyes that he remembered to be quite vulnerable, and the way her words were spoken coolly that carried that subtle, but noticeable, detachment that this thing was merely artificial. The soul of his daughter was to remain forever separated. Black clouds cut across the sky. The metallic liquid crept slowly up Herbert's body in the cantina. He shed a tear when he realized the work and effort attempted to bring her back was only in vain.

He awoke in his laboratory. His glassy eyes turned, peering over the cot at the steel-blue emergency lights that ran along a lit path toward the hallway. His mind raced with dozens of theories but one precedented thought, buried deep within the cavities, surfaced; she was *dead*. Even though his life had been devoted to his research, to his dreams with her, and to the Cloud, there was no escaping it. The possession of such power and control was incurable. Something no one should be allowed to hold. He saw it slowly consuming the swell of his own being. He could never forget her, and he could never bring her back. With that revelation, he rose from the bed and made his way to the mainframe room. To Evie.

Dozens of security guards loaded their equipment at the sight of flashing red lights and marched in succession down the labyrinthian halls. The guards reached the end of the long hall. The only door to the mainframe room was bolted and blocked tight. They proceeded to break it down.

The green oval hue of the monitor reflected in Herbert's bloodshot eyes. "Herbert." Evie said indifferently. The monitor dimmed as the pixelated eye looked away. He heard the guards outside. There wasn't much time remaining. They would break in soon and seize him. The company could continue with no interference and the inevitable power of the Cloud would be fully realized. Herbert knew it all had to be destroyed, that none of it should exist, not now, not ever. Yet, he hesitated. He hesitated to tear the wires away, to burn the drives, and to kill Evelyn. *A machine*, he tried to remind himself. *It's just a machine!* He remained immobilized, unable to carry through. "I understand, Herbert," she said. The monitor's oval eyes returned to look at him, and, as if saying goodbye, the machine began to format itself, wiping away insurmountable amounts of data directly connected to the Cloud. "Goodbye, Evie." Trembling, he watched the machine spark and catch fire behind the green hue. Then, an ageless voice in the darkness spoke, "We're not through yet, Herbert." His mild-green eyes turned crimson as wavering curtains encompassed his vision and Evie faded away.

YEAR: 2032   **DAY: 231 of 232**

EPISODE 73

The cabin is by the tracks, and it always has been. The flicker of lamplight is the only sign of life for those who travel by twilight and expect to find the ghost; they call him the Conductor. He's not here or there. He's the perfect middle man.

They watch me through a broken window pane. There's no sense in bothering an apparition. They fear me for being one. Why not leave well-enough alone? I've put the kettle on, and there's only enough water left for me.

Beyond that window lies a spirit in the witching hour of the night. He's not lurking, in search of making contact, but instead he's confined to the rundown cabin. The use of his right leg was put into practice indeed. He hobbles about the rooms inside; a cane aids him when the pain is too much to bear.

My leg has seen better nights. Most of those nights were during the Great Rebellion. The Monarch City was a sight to see before it came to rubble. My cane, my clothes, and a small pack of books was all I took with me when I fled. I didn't make this trip alone, oh no. She helped me. As She helped every character she forged.

Some say that in his beard he hides a record of the Monarch government. A record that could condemn the spirit of any body that lived within the city walls. There's no telling what he might do if prodded. Many have thrown rocks from the other side of the tracks and smashed his windows. They never crossed the tracks, mind you. And they probably never will.

If those watching me, from the woods on the other side of the tracks, only knew my purpose. The one I discovered when She discovered me. I feel they would put down their rocks, stop hiding, and come to aid this old man in his journey. But even if explained, they may see my task as frivolous and without a proper ending.

There's much to understand when your life is not only spawned into existence out of thin air, but your destiny is also laid before you. In that way I feel thankful that I have this old cabin by the tracks to keep me separated from the rest of the world until I understand. There's much to be joyous about with this lamplight inside and the twilight outside.

The legend of the Conductor says that he comes out at twilight. It's then that he waits for the train. It may never arrive. But he waits, and checks his watch. And listens.

YEAR: 2032   *DAY: -14 of 232*

EPISODE 74

Hello Old Friend,

There are those who will be entangled by vines of ivy. The Cloud is a mighty force with an army of many. But fear not when entering the black void, the place of serenity. Those who have come before and fought the Great Wars rest there, and their people will one day be reunited. Their sacrifice is the melody of battle which the wind carries through the cities for all to hear and those who choose to rise.

-    Ω

Herbert found himself fully awake in a room that he had recognized. It was a room he had been in before, but only a few times. And all those times were in dreams with Evie. The room was gargantuan and vacant, except for the throne and the corpse resting on it. Red curtains encompassed a section of the wall. The melody of classical music drifted aimlessly through the air with no purpose. *Evie, are you with me?* He wondered. But there was nothing; nothing except the chair and the music. The music was felt in-between the dust and atmosphere that surrounded his wrinkled face.

He moved closer to the throne. It was painful for him to move at all. The physical shifting of his legs and arms felt like tired weights upon him. His back ached from deep contorted muscle spasms. The physical suffering was no match to the emotional distraught he felt deep behind his tired eyes that were heavy and full of loss. He wanted to cry. He wanted to release the pressure that had been building there for so many years, but he couldn't.

Beyond the wavering red curtains, indiscernible voices murmured and carried. He wondered what awaited him on the other side. He remembered in his dreams the voices weren't there but remembered dancing with Evie to the music as a spotlight shone on them. And when the song ended, she released his hand and backed away behind the drawing curtains. There was nothing behind them except black and when she seemed to dissolve into it, the curtains receded. He recalled the melody lingered on.

He approached the throne and recognized a companion. *Theo, my God! What has happened to you? I'm sorry. I'm so sorry. This world of lies we forged is unstoppable. The cruelty of life is death. It's not just apparent death, but the death we burden one another to carry.* His thoughts grew weak and tired. He *remembered* when he was young, the energy and effort he put into great sciences. Then, an image was given to him; Evie and his wife sitting beyond the curtain in certain black. His actions had unintended consequences that ripped tears from his eyes, and which ran down his withered face.

He arose as the curtains tautly drew back. And instead of certain black, there was an empty auditorium with velvet plush seats. The murmuring voices continued from the empty seats. A Tufts Blue spotlight turned on, as all other lights faded. Herbert stepped past the curtain into it. He desired a release from the guilt and pain but found that there was none.

Looking around, the voices had settled in and the overture slowly ended. Leaning on the balcony's arm, he saw Evie and his wife. The curtains receded, closing on them.

YEAR: 2032   **DAY: 231 of 232**

EPISODE 75

I feel like the Trojan Horse, from the Greek myth. Except instead of the city of Troy, it's the Monarch City. And I'm not a wooden horse, but the last one standing of the Outsiders in this realm.

I wasn't shaken by what I saw before, but I felt uneasy at the thought of what may be below my feet. The water levels in the sewer were rising by the minute, and I have to find the source of the flooding. I came to the end of the tunnel, checking right, checking left, and it was then that I felt the calm of Her spirit come to me.

Since the fall of the city, I occasionally felt Her ghost join me in the physical realm. Her spiritual presence brought about a sense of calm. I was able to focus better, sense my surroundings with the keen insights of the creatures that crowded me in these pipes, and I garnered a steady hand with my EBS. It was standard issue: Electric Bo Staff. I stole it off one of the Monarch bounty hunters in a brief skirmish at the other end of the tunnel. I managed to steal his staff and send them both floating downstream.

Zzzzttt-CLICK! At the press of a button, the single, two-foot bar in my hand extended to a full six feet. Its structure was solid in my grip. Its composition was a mix of iron and steel; the two welded together to form a heavy design. I readied my staff at the sound of bubbling coming from below my feet. It was then, at that immediate discovery, that the CyberGator raised its snout from the filthy water at my feet and I was catapulted into the tunnel before me.

I landed against the side wall, quickly taking grip so as to not fall back in the sewage. A wave of water rushing toward me only meant that the CyberGator was not about to let me get away. It raised its snout again, *SNAP-CHOMP!* The creature's ivory fangs shined in the dim light, pasted in the slimy water of the tunnel. I quickly raised my bo staff, stopping its line of teeth in a crooked catch. A guttural cry came from the belly of the beast. Its breath on my face, and yellow eyes daggered at mine.

This perpetual stalemate was taking away what physical strength I had left. It forced me to change my footing, and that allowed my head to partially enter the CyberGator's mouth. It was then that Her ghost returned to me in a silent whisper. My emotions found a quiet moment of release. My physical strength felt renewed. She demanded that I rely on my chakra. I knew She was right. I let go of my own worldly abilities and allowed the spirits to fuel my hidden powers. With one hand on the bo staff, I twisted it sharply and broke the creature's neck. And its mutated body fell back into the waters from whence it came.

YEAR: 2032   **DAY: -13 of 232**

EPISODE 76

The revolving stairs led up the increasingly narrow tower. Upon each floor, Norman found a candle burning inside a lantern, with the excess wax dripping down to the water-logged floorboards. Every room was unique in its design and contained very few objects or furniture. In the first room, he found painted portraits on the walls. They were Biblical ones; of a garden, of the Flood, and the Crucifixion.

He ascended. In the second room was a bare table with a projector on it that played. Home images showed Norman as a child in the backyard of his parents' suburban house. It was a summer day and his mother wore sunglasses, as his father captured her on film. She turned away shyly and used her hand to motion the camera toward Norman who played by the inflatable pool. The footage looped. Norman was unable to summon this memory on his own.

He continued up.

An overwhelming anxiety formed in the pit of his stomach. This place caused a tension that knotted his mind, making it feel it wasn't his own anymore. The splotches of dark purple seemed to gather territory over his body, and he felt the signs of a fever ensue. *Perhaps this is a dream*, he thought. But he couldn't shake himself awake. He was trapped in the conduit of this museum for some unknown purpose.

The storm raged on outside. He could see the waters rising, engulfing the previous floors.

The third floor contained a spinning carousel lantern that projected shadowed figurines onto the walls. On the table by the window there were two perfectly symmetrical halves of an elephant. One half was red and white in color, the other half was blue and black. Norman approached them, picking them up. Connecting the pieces together caused the lantern to surge, blinding the room in white light. Then, dimming back, the carousel brought forth life. The shadows manipulated into movement and danced a macabre ritual; rising from the shadowed ground grew a long and slender serpent who offered the figures a telescope to view the stars. When they did, their bodies ascended into the heavens and belonged to them.

A soft and tender voice whispered into the room and Norman, at once, felt a sense of peace wash over him. The wind gently caressed his hand and led him to the top of the lighthouse. *Her* presence was undeniable. Even in nightmares *She* was immune and came to those who were lost.

Norman stood against the metal railing feeling the gushing wind whip his body with great force. The ocean surrounded the lighthouse and stretched infinitely, mirroring the immense sea of stars hanging above him in the heavens. In the grave distant horizon, there was a cliffside and *She* stood there. Ivy vines that grew around the tower spiraled up and wrapped the railing. In their entanglement lay a child's yellow kaleidoscope. Without hesitation or fear, Norman untangled the toy and peered into the swirling vortex of abstract colors and shapes towards the cliffside.

YEAR: 2032   **DAY: Unknown**

EPISODE 77

The swivel chair was gone. I was no longer sitting, but standing in a stairwell of a strange apartment building. The place was unknown to me, but once this reality snapped into existence it felt as though I was finishing a step of my foot in front of the other. I looked down to stop myself from tripping. I have never been here before.

Compelled by fear, I quickly charged upward to the top of the stairwell. I couldn't stop, my heart racing, no means of escape as I passed each floor to notice not a single entrance or exit from this labyrinth. The stairs twisted and turned, feeling like a hamster wheel designed by the Devil himself.

Then I discovered the top. The banister was made of marble, slick and stylishly designed in a square cut that met the only door I've seen in my marathon up the stairs. The handle was bright red, opposite the charcoal color of the door itself. There was no time for admiration, so I quickly took note of its location to the rest of the steps below and opened it. The creak of the door frightened me, hoping that this was not some sinister trick of Zenith's to put me in a hallucination only to lead me back to him.

But I entered a quiet hallway instead. No longer than twenty feet long with no windows for greater bearings, I paced quickly to the only door available to me. It opened, but on a compressed-hinge for controlled swaying. It felt like some of the compression units inside myself. I took note of its design and felt the mechanics because I, too, am half to their being. I remembered that when I entered the apartment.

I was sweating. To this expression of reality, I quickly found a hand towel draped over the handlebar of the apartment's kitchen stove. I dried my face and neck, turning to view the place simultaneously. Everything in its place. A wall-TV. Modern furniture upon a wooden floor. There was a suspended patio where through its glass door you could look out and see a blurry rendition of the Monarch City. And a smudge on that glass door. I inspected the smudge closer to see small fragments of bird feathers. They were bright red streaks of feather.

YEAR: 2032   *DAY: -12 of 232*

EPISODE 78

Across the great divide and separated by the vast unknowable planes that exist, the two lovers wait, hopeful to be reunited. The Lighthouse sigil pierces through the night sky, only to be swallowed by the reign of the Cloud. Yet, behind their eyes the message is transmitted and received.

"What are we doing here, Laura?" said an agitated Griswald. His projection flickered from a weakened signal. I stood at the edge of the cliff staring out into the arctic waters that were upset. I can't say exactly what it was that drew me to the edge of the cliff, or what part of the ferocious push and pull of the tide that called to me, other than a sense of déjà vu. I looked out over the restless waves, into the thick Cumulonimbus. The towering vertical cloud flashed rays of light within its cluster. The eye of the storm was approaching, and it would hit *strong* and *fast*. But there was something else in it, a sense I gathered from observing it at such a close exposure. There was a mist in the air as the swirling vortex roared over the chilled waters.

Although the cluster of this strange cloud formed alone, it had now gathered an army, and the squall line marched ahead of the cold front. The light flashed again. It seemed an odd peculiarity. I set my wristwatch and decided to document the pattern.

"You need to leave now, Laura! You're standing in the goddam center of this thing!"

"There's something strange about the light flashes. I don't know. It looks like a pattern."

"It's just lightning."

"Don't be naïve, Griswald. I know you *have to* see it too, it's not just lightning."

"Don't be stubborn, Laura!" You're in d—" The signal died, and the projection jumbled static before cutting out completely. I continued taking my observations.

A strong gust of wind flared from behind me. It rolled over the cliffside without a warning. I was jotting the last few numbers down when the gale-force winds sent me just over the edge. My body tumbled, smashing against the jagged rock. I balled up and caught something to hold onto. The wind continued in a furry as my body knocked against the rock. I leaned into the cove of the cliff and waited for the wind to settle.

Climbing back up, I collected my things and made my way back to the vehicle.

There was a message waiting for me, "You have a-*static*-from Theodore Brimley, would y-*static*- listen?" The conditions made Theo's message near impossible to decipher. I could tell by his tone it seemed urgent. I rushed back to the hotel to find it empty and Theo's luggage gone. I sat on the edge of the bed and nervously listened to the message in full. Outside the window, the sky darkened as the storm approached.

EPISODE 79

I awoke from my dream and now stood inside the quietest room in the world. It appeared to be crafted in wood, designed with a homey comfort in mind. It was a scientific experiment of anechoic room simulation but with shaped timber to allow the subject inside it to feel a form of nostalgia simultaneously. I remember this because of a previous homicide investigation I performed while working in the Monarch City years ago. The victim of that case was found in one of these rooms.

The beach was gone, the waves ceased. The sultry sound of my wife's voice was lost somewhere outside of here. I was not dreaming anymore, although this chamber felt like a dream. The floor, ceiling, and walls are the same. Sanded pine and its aroma are still potent from however long ago the tree they chose was cut. I was tempted to reach out and touch it. And when I did, there appeared a screen that overtook a single wall. Its texture felt that of a bedsheet, dipped in a silver wax. I was confused by its presence but welcomed the warmth it shared when a bright light illuminated from inside.

At first, I covered my eyes as a precaution from the blinding beam of light that pulsed from the silver screen in front of me. The deprivation of sound made the sight of this unidentified thing that much more horrifying. I screamed but not a sound left my vocal cords, not even an inhale or exhale of oxygen which I continued to guess at how I was receiving it. The screen gave no assistance in my subdued thoughts and lent no knowledge to the mystery of me inside the quietest room in the world. But I allowed it to have me.

I lowered my arm from covering my eyes and allowed the light to shine against my face. The glow of the screen was reduced to a hot smolder that was visible only by an incoming transmission. Power was building from behind the screen and I could feel its warmth. A sound had finally snuck into the room, but it was hushed almost immediately. A small crackle, like fire traveling through a hollowed log. I thought I felt my heart faint, but it was my imagination, my anxiety.

White noise protruded from the screen and formed a muffled language I could not understand. The terror I experienced was met with a dubious image coming from behind it. I saw a young man in a modern apartment, staring back at me. His clothes torn and revealed several wounds made up of skin and electrical parts. I reached for the wall again, hoping that he would reach back.

YEAR: 2032   **DAY: -11 of 232**

EPISODE 80

For the first time in a long while, I felt cold. Listening to the message over and over, I found myself adrift in familiar tides. It was becoming increasingly frequent for Theo to leave because of the Company. While he embraced these disruptions, I was left to accept them. How easy it was for these distractions to enter into our lives, uproot and upheave our time, of which we shared very little. It's easy to notice distance forming, but what it *can do*, or what it *will do* is yet to be seen. A myriad of thoughts raced through my mind. I packed my remaining things and left for home. The coldness I felt only continued to fester.

For some reason that morning came to mind. Something I hadn't thought about, but now it lingered. I had awoken from a nightmare. The details of it I don't wish to recall. It was rare to have such surreal dreams again. The last one I can remember vividly was when I was a child. And, perhaps, that is why that morning came to mind. Although I feel this isn't true. Waking up in a new apartment felt like starting over, if only we did. The thermostat was broken and inside it was sixty-two degrees.

There grew an uncomfortable silence between us, a stalemate of conversations. I believe it was that morning that I became sure of it. It had been bothering me that we weren't really talking through things anymore.

The shades of blue projected onto the wall, but within their sublime shading I noticed an imperfection, a smudge of some kind that existed. I swiped my hand as the next darker shade took form, yet there it was again. The smudge. It was in the same spot on the wall. I wondered what it was, and why it was there. I hadn't noticed it before. This thing, whatever it is— "Laura!" *—was it growing? I swiped and the next shade projected onto the wall.*

I was on the next available flight home. When I arrived back in the city, I took a cab. My head lay against the window watching; the advertising city lights, a crowd of people exiting the theater, and the complex chaotic lives fluttering about all just beyond the thin pane of glass. At the red-light intersection, a street performer played the cello. Those passing by ignored the man and his music.

I told Theo the movers were coming, but he knew this from our discussion the night before. I swiped again finding a vivid teal shading. My eyes scoured the wall for the smudge, which existed in every shade before except this one. This time it wasn't there, and, for a moment, my mind seemed to rest easy at this assurance. "What about this shade? It feels pleasant, doesn't it?" I asked. "Sure," he said swiftly. He gathered his things and left without saying goodbye.

That hadn't been the first time we left things unsaid between us, and it wasn't our last. I remember approaching the wall, feeling drawn in. I extended my hand, slowly placing it on the spackled teal. To my revelation, I saw it. The smudge had returned.

YEAR: 2032   **DAY: 64 of 231**

EPISODE 81

She may not have had her father present in the physical life, but I certainly did not feel an obligation to take his place. His spirit was alive in her during the training, and I saw the reflection of his personality in her eyes. She will make the End a joyous thing.

I was glad to have left the sewers. But coming upon the Mind Trap Chamber was a fear I've never felt before. I could see the tall candelabras on either side of the door that kept the Chamber secure. Eternal flames, lit by the spirits that inhabit the room. I saw no need in being cautious, the Chamber called out to me and knew my presence before I made it to the end of the hall.

I took in the craftmanship of the door. Great oak mixed with wild cherry trim, and steel bolts and plates to harness a strength in homage to the Nordic ancestral gods. To take in its beauty in a reality in which technology is so advanced and great, left me with a bite of nostalgia that soon loosened my inhibitions and allowed the darkened Mind Trap to begin its first phase. I dropped my pack, my Bo staff, and removed my harem pants and shoes. It was time to present myself to this covenant and be washed clean to enter the plane in which She inhabits.

I chose to sit cross-legged and with straight posture, a humble position I felt for such a foreboding god of darkness. The Mind Trap was mixed in the lore of the Monarch, the deity that a secret sect known as the Red Eyes were known to have started worshipping before they built the empire that we would come to know as the Monarch City. The purpose of this Trap was to enslave any mind that dared to enter free will. And in this chamber before me now, is complete slavery.

The quiet of the hall was my last drop of pleasure before the inevitable door would open and I would enter a reality without any control of my own. And I used this time to meditate. That's when I heard his voice. Her father's voice. It came to me like a cold wind of reality, but hidden inside it was the strength of a dream. Marlon's timbre voice, "You have come so far, William. Your physical body has changed so much since the start of your training. And your purpose is feverishly strong. I thought it complete when you rescued Clarice. You trained my daughter well. May your mind heal through this process. Don't think it a trap once inside."

His compliment made me cry in the stillness before the door of the Mind Trap. The demonic presence of that hall and Chamber mocked my tears. In Marlon's encouragement, I believe to have found the key to my survival of the Mind Trap. And the door opened. I smiled to welcome my fate and its captors, and wiped the tears away.

YEAR: 2032   **DAY: -10 of 232**

EPISODE 82

An ocean of clear, reflective glass lay below my feet. A trepidation deters my step, even though my body feels weightless. I am surrounded by a thinly formed fog, and there is nothing in this place, except the chilling touch from the breeze nudging me forward.

With one foot suspended, gravity is my momentum pushing me back down. The grass forms around my feet, feeling different somehow. Some reason existed, this I was sure of, but one that I was unable to understand fully and purely only felt. I knelt down, running my hands through the grass feeling each rigid blade between my fingers. Then, I pressed the palm of my hand down to the Earth. The rough terrain pricked my senses. I felt the pebbles in the soil, the insects that moved, and the Earth breathing.

The artificial moon's gaze shone bright, and the perfect balance of stars shined like scattered crystals in the dark sea above. All of it had been fabricated cleverly. Behind the moon's shadow there was a layer of something. A second moon, one so transparent that it was nearly invisible to the naked eye. As I caught its glimpse and became aware of its bizarre presence, it crystallized into focus and seemed to draw from my consciousness, becoming opaquer. The anomaly was unexplainable. *Was this part of the artificial projection, or could it be that Earth's moon still existed?*

I hastily made my way inside to grab my camera and loaded it with film. Upon my return, a chariot of dark clouds roared closer. I removed the lens cap and pulled the Shadowed Moon into sharp focus. The sky flickered, as if frames of film were cut from the sky, encompassing the world around me into a static moment of complete darkness. I took another still with my camera, then another. I felt myself being carried away into someplace else. My vigor was renewing from this discovery, and so was the Shadowed Moon, which increased in luminescence.

I remember as a child being enamored by the wondrous cosmos, and the sublime nature of their perfection. They often instilled me with a sense of peace and serenity even in moments of fear. Something I never felt from the artificial projections that were created to take their place. When the sky and moon ceased to exist, a void opened. A void that was felt by everyone. And in it The Cloud came to be.

Dark clouds covered the Shadowed Moon and the horizon prematurely lightened with the forthcoming sun.

A turquoise light emitted from my arm. I glanced at my watch. An incoming call from Griswald flashed. I accepted and launched the projection. He visualized in the grass. His dour demeanor was unchanged from when we last spoke. "I've been trying to reach you. I had no idea what happened to you. I should've known you'd make it out alive though. You're as reckless as you are determined."

"Have you called just to reprimand my character?"

His manner turned grim. "No. I need you to come into the office straight away. There have been some peculiar anomalies detected that we need to discuss at once."

YEAR: 2032   *DAY: 65 of 231*

EPISODE 83

There is fog in the mind. And She is calling out for those who need freedom.

There was one last patch of green just outside the city wall. A culmination of scorched blades comprised of what little photons the plants could get through a smoky sky. To cut the blades would be a damaging blow to the soul, and snuff out what color the Monarch City had left. Zenith contemplated the existence of this grass and what purpose it served him as he bled out on a toppled battlement that fell with him during the invasion.

Being on the opposing side, the losing side, of such a fight was something he already accepted. The laser blast in his side, an open wound still killing him. Zenith never saw such rage before. He remembered the eyes of the rebels who attacked. Their fury gave him strength for the commands he gave out to his men. He was determined to protect the city, his men, and the entity that he believed would save humanity.

The Cloud was a system to him. It gave him serenity and comfort to know that there was an order to how he could remember, dream, and aspire to do more in the world around him. Its destruction meant snuffing out the color of his world.

To vanquish such a god in his life would mean that he would have to imagine alone, without inspiration, without control. This fueled the fight in him, until the end.

He had no wife, no children of his own, but there was a family in the beginning. The early days of building the city alongside another soldier, Marlon. They met during recruitment, and enlisted the same day. They ate together, drank together, and through their daily regime of work they got to know each other. Zenith met his daughter, Clarice, and his wife, Star, for which she made meals for them both to take to the factories as the city continued to expand over the years. Together, they never stopped working.

The patch of grass came into focus once more for Zenith. It was then that the thoughts of his betrayal seeped in with a fury of their own. The murderous feelings crept back into his heart. Fire, blood, and ash. He sobbed there on the fallen battlement, feeling his heart begin to pump as hard as it could. It started to hurt worse than the wound in his side. Its throbbing and pulling inside his chest made his crying and gasping for breath an ugly sight if anyone should come upon him. But he was alone. And there, under a burned banner of the Monarch insignia, he took his last breath and entered the afterlife as a traitor and murderer.

YEAR: 2032   *DAY: -9 of 232*

EPISODE 84

I step forward into the unknowable plane that lay in front of me. The fog kindly wraps around me, and I feel its static charge prick my body. This ethereal plane beckons me toward the future, and toward the end.

Death was certain. It might've been a few months. It could've been up to a year. But it was at a great unease that the doctor assured Laura's mother it was certain that her husband wouldn't have long to live. The cancer was stage IV, and uncontrollably spreading. The doctor had suggested a new, untested procedure as an alternative. Laura's father refused. He rather death take him when it was his time.

Both Laura's parents sat her down and explained things to her, just as the doctor had explained it to them. They saw no use of lying to their daughter and prepared her for the immediate realization of death. Laura handled it as well as expected. She remained quiet, inert, and her eyes lingered on her father. He was a tough man, and one of plain features and candid expressions. She knew he loved her because she heard him say it once before. Not many times after that, as she came to think about it. She felt the warmth of the sun rest easy against her back when they told her. Her parents never made a habit to lie to her. It was to her own benefit they'd argue. One she may not fully comprehend as a child but would as an adult, especially if she had children of her own. And it was her parents' belief to treat Laura as an adult, even if she wasn't yet.

Neither her mother nor father cried, showed anger, or fear when explaining; there was simply nothing expressed at all. It was as if any emotional layers that might have been felt were shed from them, and these new forms, these hollow, inert individuals sitting a measly foot apart from each other, were the fossilized remains of life. When they finished, they asked Laura if she understood. She shrugged, then nodded soberly. A vacuum of silence lingered. She took a breath, paused, and felt the steady rhythmic flow of her heartbeat. Then she asked, "Will I ever have a sibling?"

She grew up wondering how different things might have been if she had a sibling. A brother or sister, she didn't prefer one over the other, just someone else with her. Being an only child sometimes felt like solitary confinement. She started speaking less and less, and after the death of her father, she seldom spoke at all. Everything began processing internally for Laura, and if she spoke it was only after she realized, to a fault, she was in grave trouble with a teacher, her mother, or some adult authority. Her mind wrapped around the notion of *explanation. Everything,* she thought*, was explainable.* She found some things she couldn't explain, but mostly this involved people. People were hard to understand, hard to interpret. Their actions varied from person to person, so did their intentions and emotions. Some chose to lie, while others told the truth. Some chose to believe in things that were scientific fact, while others believed in faith of unseen things.

But there was something she couldn't explain. Her *dreams*. She had wonderfully vivid ones, and horrendously frightening ones. When she awoke, she could remember the tiniest of details, down to nearly the temperature itself. These dreams were entire worlds, lived in, fully realized, and quite often, she discovered, were populated with strange and charming characters.

Bizarrely, she had dreams that she was the wind itself. These were her favorite. Wrapping softly at a window or pulling a stranger away from the Shadows that infested the dreamworlds. She looked for the Shadows in the real world. Her curiosity teeming with wonder, her hands pulsing with excitement, but she never found them. This enemy's presence was only in dreams. *When one sleeps, the Shadows awaken.* When she was the wind, she had a freedom that was boundless, which was a desirable pleasure not attainable when being awake. The real world was a constricting plateau, confined to a physical body and its senses, but as the wind she was free to roam. An island in the South Pacific Ocean captured her imagination. It was a barren sanctuary of ruins, untouched and uninhabited, serene and safe. But here, she was still alone. Isolated in a void of silence.

YEAR: 2016

EPISODE 85

No one controls their story anymore. And because of that, we lose our spirit.

The waiting room was the same. Bland, colorless, procedural. The familiarity of it still felt new somehow. It had an odorless, clean smell to it and the feeling prompted a tinge of anxiety in the back of my mind. Which is where I was. I was in the back of my mind. I travelled through the cosmos, through planes that were thought not to exist, and I worked through simulation after simulation to get here. It took some time, to say the least.

I felt I could look at my reflection in the decorative mirror across the room for the rest of the day. But that nostalgic impulse faded quickly when I remembered my mission, and knew how little time I had left to complete it. Still, I saw what time travel and human aging had done to my external self. I wanted to feel young again, look young again. But that girl was lightyears in the past, passive in everything she did.

The doctor was in. And besides me, there only seemed to be one other patient: a man with blue hair and round spectacles who sat in a metal folding chair in the corner. He was watching me past those tinted glasses, but kept pretending to flip through a digital magazine he took from the nearby end table. He looked at me as if he knew me. But the vengeance in my heart that brought me to this point in time led me to think I didn't even know myself.

"Clarice?" The doctor peered through a crack in the door. He was ready for me. And judging by the smile on his face, the erasing of his memory of me worked like a charm. Those stained canines still flashed at me as I walked into the room, casually. I gave no reason for him to suspect I was there for any other purpose than for a scanning. I saw the chair in which I sat, the helmet that was once placed on my head. And the doctor quickly fell into the same swivel chair he used that day long ago.

I wasted no time. I pulled out the laser pistol that was given to me, pointed it at his face. He turned from his clipboard to stare down the barrel of my gun. Shock took over his face until I freed the information from my subconscious and downloaded it to his. Then there was terror. He knew who I was now. Why I was there. "Do you mean to shoot me? Retribution for me simply doing my duty?" He asked nervously. I shook my head, almost laughed at the loneliness I felt in this task. I controlled everything and it felt empty. I motioned the weapon for him to get up, and I pointed to the chair with the scanning helmet. "There. Take a seat. And think on this: Supernova and I are now one."

YEAR: 2032   **DAY: 34 of 231**

EPISODE 86

Ironically, the laugh track from the once endearing and beloved family-friendly black and white situational-dramedy series *Family Habits* paraded around the expanse of the old maple-wood home as Wallaby Huckles Wuxler attempted in short and feeble bursts of energy to open the mason jar of homemade peanut butter that his mother sent him with an attached note of parental guilt-tripping to 'please come visit soon'. The sound of laughter reverberated and amplified off the metallic lamp shades and indented thick-cut maple wood cubby-holes and open-ceiling floor plan and myriad of shimmering windows with tan sheer curtains and hanging kitchen *Luminecente* brand pots and pans, which filled most of the cabinet space and now overflowed to hang above the granite island in the center of the kitchen, until it finally rang deep within the hollows of Wallaby's ear drum. He struggled. Unable with the purest intentions to curb his increasingly growing hunger for which he had already missed breakfast, a rare occurrence, and went straight for an early lunch. After a few more arduous albeit forlorn attempts the vacuum-sealed lid of the mason jar proved to stymie W.H.W.'s roaring hunger. The wall television plays as part of the minimum six hours that Wallaby will consume today.

A simple snack of *Cheese Blitz*, a highly concentrated deep-fried cheese wrapped around more cheese, will suffice in the meantime. Wallaby is of a stocky build with quite an unusual gibbous shape on the top of his head and physically larger than his father and brothers and his father's brothers with an average intelligence when compared to the standard individual, but a seemingly lower intelligence when compared to his own family of creative geniuses. His younger brother, Blithe, for example became an award winning author at the age of thirteen for an opus that far exceeded three-thousand pages and was hailed by many critics as "the greatest book ever written"; his older brother, Baron, had become a renowned pilot in the military's air force branch which dropped "the bomb" to annihilate a presumed threat which was speculated to ignite the next world war thus saving and preventing the sweep of superfluous fear from rising amongst the nations; his pseudo-talented auteur father, Bjorn, had a collection of independent and studio works ranging from documentaries, tv shows (including *Family Habits*) and features which built a lasting and wealthy legacy mostly overseas where his work was most famous until the eventual "bomb" wiped out his most beloved fandom; his radiantly charming mother, Winnipeg, – for which she was named after the place she was born – propelled to stardom as a kitchen connoisseur of lavish original cooking and eventually kitchen appliances and even products (including her widely known *Luminecente* brand which key feature was their lasting durability) and who now resided in a European coastal town; and finally his uncle, Warland, a masterfully obstinate painter and humanitarian whose most famous abstract works (including *Le Témoin, L´oeil*, and *L´esclave*) sold upwards of ten million dollars collectively and whose name and body of work is the axiom of "pure art" now taught in every school; needless to say Wallaby's family had somehow limitless potential in creative endeavors except for Wallaby himself whose main function within the family unit boiled down to first consumer. Wallaby ate more *Cheese Blitz* as his stomach twisted in discomfort from the lack of something more sustainable.

Within the vast sanctuary of his home lied every family member's work ever contrived, whether finished or unfinished, and now the walled television played rerun episodes of *Family Habits* before inevitably switching to the unsuccessful spinoff series *Family Shenanigans* or the even less successful remake of *Family Habits* produced fifteen years after the original series ended all while Wallaby sat rereading the guilt-ridden letter from his mother which also reminded him, the letter did, that his presence was mandatory at next year's Wuxler Gala in which all Wuxler clans from around the globe would seethe and breathe in close proximities while ignoring their common-enough family feuds all to entertain the notion of a wealthy and stable and happy "All-American" family image – which they in fact were a mixed-melting pot of multi-ethnic genealogy – to be broadcast nationally, and, in fact, this year Wallaby was actually given the reasonably important task of choosing the caterer for such an occasion. It was here, amongst the myriad of family history and entertainment at his disposal, that Wallaby contemplated the rest of his day and how his time would be best spent for which he had no discernable inclination. He muted the television. A refulgence of silence captured the room except for the gooey sounds W.H.W.'s mouth made while eating *Cheese Blitz*, followed by the singing sounds his stomach made in constipation.

YEAR: 2032   **DAY: 323**

EPISODE 87

They haven't left the apartment in days. It seemed as though they were trapped there. The doors were locked, thick metal for protection with attached wooden panels for style. Syfus thought nothing of it, having seen the inside of the Monarch City prison system. But Roger, he was questioning everything about his surroundings. Not just how he got there, but why they couldn't leave.

The oddest thing of their current environment was not just the familiarity of it, but the view from the apartment balcony. Through the glass sliding door there was nothing to be seen. A wavy mirage-like glare had fixed itself on the pane. Staring out had left both of them with only a blurry reflection of themselves. Yet somehow, they could tell there was a world beyond the glass door.

Roger threw down the last card from his hand into the pile between him and Syfus. He couldn't handle being cooped up like this for very much longer. He stroked the back of his neck, anxiously. There was no purpose for them that could be served while stuck here in someone else's place of living. So, he searched for clues. It was one drawer after another; coming up with either a typical utensil, household item, or something just as bland and useless as the thing before it.

Syfus followed Roger's lead, mocking him at first in retaliation for quitting the game in which he had a better hand. But the mocking dissipated at the sight of an obscure item in the first drawer he opened. The skeleton of a female bird, on its side and bones in perfect form. This triggered a memory for Roger as he joined Syfus at the find.

"That's a painted pig as if I'd ever seen one", Roger said, cigarette plucked between his lips and lit before he finished the comment.

"It means nothing, detective." Syfus closed the drawer.

"What do you mean, nothing?

"It's without purpose."

"YOU'RE WITHOUT PURPOSE!" Roger childishly open-ed the drawer again and grabbed the remains of the bird and threw it at Syfus.

Knock, Knock. It came from the apartment door. Roger and Syfus looked to each other and froze. Time stopped. They were unable to move. It seemed like a spell had come over them. The knocking continued. Roger was able to crack his lips, "Who's there?", his eyes blinking uncontrollably as he watched the door.

YEAR: 2032   **DAY: -6 of 232**

EPISODE 88

Staring out the boardroom window, I inhale a slow and deep breath; holding it until I feel the oxygen burn against my lungs, until I feel the pressure building in my head, until my vision starts to eclipse like the iris of an aperture, until this ghostly apparition of virga from a low Nimbostratus Cloud spawning snow ceases. I force my eyes shut. It has been exactly five months and fourteen days since I received the call that shook the very foundation of my world.

Bzz. Bzzzzz.

What is that sound? I open my eyes spotting a monstrous hive just outside the window in the upmost corner of the glass. Chaotically charged, the aggressive hornets swarm over one another in a unified batch, completely covering their vertical nest. The sound returns, humming and prodding in my ear. Its buzzing grows deafening, thunderous, filling the silence of this room. Through the slits in the ceiling vent, I see the infiltrating swarm.

With the tick of the thermostat engaging, the hornets in the ceiling are gone. A cool rush of air is sent into the boardroom of Cloud Tech. The slight chill gains territory of my body, crawling up my arm, trying to manipulate my emotions, a full-on assault of neural stimuli in my head. It seems to work against my desire as goosebumps begin to form. Standing here, in the place Theo once worked tirelessly at, brings back so many memories. Most of them I don't wish to recall.

This monolithic building, the tallest in the world by far, soars high above the city directly into the patch of Nimbostratus clouds. The boardroom is mostly comprised of characterless features; employing the bulky-standard solid dark cherry conference table, Bankers Lamps evenly spaced every few feet, plush black office chairs, and bare chestnut colored paneled-walls along the side of which I was escorted in and leads back towards the company's waiting pods. The only features that did provide character to the room were its remaining two glass walls, which diagonally enclose in on each other forming a triangular floor made of thick, clear glass, of which you can't even see the ground below. A patient of vertigo would last point-three seconds before having a massive panic attack in the room.

That day, five months and fourteen days ago, I received a call from an unknown number, an employee from Cloud Tech, who informed me there had been an accident involving Theo. The details were shallow, and I wasn't allowed to see him until weeks later. Finally, that moment arrived. I saw his body perfectly still in the bed as tubes and monitors showed vital signs, the bare minimum of life while he remained so far away. Months passed without improvement or hope that he would awaken.

The interim... has come and gone in a flash, a blur of eclipsing moments consisting of life and events and emotions and decisions and people who tell you 'they're there for you' when in actuality they can't be because they don't know what it's like to be in your situation, but they say it anyway for some reason, perhaps to somehow feel better themselves but I don't know... I just want to understand them. I just want, desperately more than anything, to not be me for a moment, so I can have release from this pain.

He passed when I saw him today in the hospital. In the room, there was something *uncanny* about him, something I hadn't caught before. His opened palm was cool and stiff in mine.

YEAR: 2032   **DAY: 232 of 232**

EPISODE 89

Too many times had the blue-haired devil stood in the corridors of my mind. He neither knocked nor called out to explain his presence to me. Was he someone mute or without hands? It wasn't until the Infinite opened that he began to knock and whisper untruths.

The vengeance left a rancid taste in the corners of my mouth. The doctor may have been a by-product of the Monarch system, but he was also a human being, in some form. Thoughts like that began to pummel me emotionally with a level of guilt I hadn't felt before. Even as I left him from the scanning room and made it back to the waiting area, I felt regret deep in the pit of my stomach. I was out of practice when it came to violence.

"You've waited a long time to do that. Haven't you, Clarice?" The reflection of my sadness reflected back into the spectacles of the blue-haired man. He was old and familiar in his usual presentation in a chair, busying himself with some other menial task. This time he continued to read from the digital magazine, flipping through page after page finding no interest in its content. "What would you know of the time I've spent here?" The guilt sagged me spiritually and physically, so I was forced to sit.

"He inflicted much pain into your life, much like the rest of the scum in the Monarch religion," he groveled.

"What would you know of the Monarch and its disturbing feats?"

"Plenty, considering I was the father of their Captain."

I was shocked, and sank deeper into the waiting area chair.

"You should worry no more of Zenith or the Monarch for that matter. Your focus should be on where you're headed now, Clarice."

"You know my name and I still don't know yours. Or what you want!"

The blue-haired devil replaced the digital magazine and dropped his spectacles on the end table with it. He rubbed his eyes, a half-yawn surprised him. "I've grown tired of waiting for you to make the right choice in this journey of yours, Clarice. You've grown and succeeded in ways that no other traveler has ever done before when diving into the belly of the Cloud. It's time."

"What does this Cloud system have to do with anything anymore? I have sunk through it, erased its memories, its data. I've now morphed it to my soul."

The old man reclaimed his spectacles, and leaned farther back into his chair. "There is much more to see in *this* Cloud, Clarice.

YEAR: 2032   **DAY: -5 of 232**

EPISODE 90

The dark clouds twisted nightmarishly, clustering into a thick swirling vortex around the lighthouse where Norman stood, kaleidoscope in hand. Through the device he peered; illuminating colors and shapes curved through the clouds towards the cliffside. But she was no longer standing there. The frozen tundra of land barren. Thunder roared and a bright flash of light struck the tower's foundation, causing Norman to stumble back. The wind ferociously whipped, pulling him from the metal platform and into the vortex. Descending rapidly, eclipsing memories of a life he *felt* were true but couldn't recall projected inside the vortex. The imagery was grainy, technicolored, and soundless. A flicker of white static lines impeded the viewing, as an indiscernible image flashed before all went dark and Norman sailed through the bottom smashing into glass.

Waking up… I felt my eyes burst open, even though they remained closed. I could feel my arms moving frantically, even though they weren't. It was a strange occurrence to feel movement inwardly through the mind when my physical self was still bound in the chair, still numb for being someplace else for so long. Slowly my body was coming back though.

The realization of cold steel compressed against my skull

came first. The scanning helmet was still on, still keeping my motor functions impaired. I fought the urge to give up. My hands rose slowly. Fighting against an unseen pressure that hung in the air as I tried to release the latch and cast the helmet aside. When the metal helmet finally struck the ground, its symbiotic associations to me were still felt. A sort of phantom sensation of the metal compressed against my skull and of my senses still feeling influenced. Could I finally be free from this trap?

The world remained blurry for several moments before my eyes could sharply focus on anything. What had I just gone through? Locked away in my subconscious were feelings and memories of so many other people. Lives that were not mine, but somehow, through some means, I was connected to them now.

I had been tempted by the power of the Cloud and the scanning helmet. I failed, falling into its trap. But, I'm back now and maybe I can find a way to stop it. There will be many who try to seize its power, but I believe this is impossible. It's far too great for anyone to control. Its purpose and inherent divinity are unimaginable.

I needed to find Laura and make sure she's safe. This thought paused me. It was in no way conjured by an external source. There was no reminder of her in the room. Yet, I realized instinctually, I thought of her. This thought also brought me much pain, and that familiar *tick* resurfaced. I had to concede that in my unwavering attempts to perfect the Cloud and focus on my work I had always cast her aside. Selfishly, I desired a natural and genuine connection as it was before, but for it to happen effortlessly.

The smell of rich tobacco struck my senses, and a twisted southern drawl spoke my name, "Welcome back, Theo."

YEAR: 2032   **DAY: 232 of 232**

EPISODE 91

There is a great distant thought begging to be captured. It is more than an idea and it lies beyond the woods. To look at one's feet is to not see what is ahead. To look to the stars is to always forget your footing. Beware, the Conductor is on the path.

The click-clack of the wheels grinding the track was at a dull roar to my ears within the fourth to last railcar. My head was starting to pound, and the thought of this journey lasting much longer sunk me in some sort of depression. There were deep, dark tunnels that added to the unfolding melancholy I was finding myself in. I kept thinking of home, where that is now for me, I do not know. I followed the blue-haired devil to the station and we climbed aboard on a whim to his words and promises.

He told me the story of the Conductor and the Cloud. Their connection was shared during the first stage of the Monarch rise to power. Once upon a time, the Conductor was a wise leader of the Monarch religion. His studies led him to a crossroads when he discovered a way to power the first Cloud. His zealous attitude towards its creation gave reason to fear him, and he was soon demoted to the Keeper of the

Cloud. He was tasked with simply watching over the systems during the midnight hours, and some say he lost his mind along with his pride during this time of change. Some believe he mutated.

Whoosh! The pilot of the train had hit an air pocket upon exiting the darkened tunnel. I was shaken and felt the trembling resound through each railcar past ours. Its engines neutralized and it began coasting down a suspended rail in the valley between two identical mountains. The conversation in which the blue-haired devil told the story of the Conductor must've transpired much earlier because it was then that I woke up to the man with blue hair staring at me from across the booth.

"We are close to him, Clarice."

"I know. I can feel him. Can you tell me what to expect of him?" I asked.

"Expect a man of few words. And even less patience for anyone attempting to understand the Cloud and its technology," he replied.

There was no sense of danger, but I continued to use the techniques Bill had taught me, and the strength and abilities my father bestowed on me to discern. I could not go into this one blind, like I did when first entering the Cloud. Since I barely survived the system of that entity, I couldn't imagine what I'd have to endure to speak to its potential creator. I feared what realities would become known to me once we meet with him. Time, space, and the spirit felt entwined and in the balance with the inevitable discussion I felt purposed to have with the Conductor.

YEAR: 2032   **DAY: -4 of 232**

EPISODE 92

The old saying goes, 'you can have all this in the palm of your hand' or 'at the touch of your fingertips'. The power it grants you is immense. And unstable. It started with an unquenchable desire. The Revolution was soon underway as the world turned. Technological advancements and futuristic ideas provided access to wonderous new amusements, but information has uncontrollably spread, becoming a micro-ocean, inflicting and growing into a forthcoming tsunami.

The rich earthy tobacco rose through the air. The smoke broke apart and faded out of existence, but the rapacious scent remained; thick, sojourned somewhere in-between the passive atmosphere of the sanguine tinted sanctuary. The Pink Cowboy straightened his bolo tie and languidly paced his steps from around a chair facing a fish tank.

The fish tank caused the only shift of color in the monochromatic room. It was a faint blue hue that seemed to flicker. It was empty inside, except for turquoise-colored rocks at the bottom that held a shimmering reflection.

"How were the waters, Theo?" The Pink Cowboy's cigarette smoldered between his bony fingers. His attentive gaze remained fixed on me. The process of conjuring an intelligent thought felt impossible to me for some reason. In that moment, I felt lobotomized, completely immobile. I perceived but could not act. I scanned the room, intaking more information around me.

With no visible windows, there were dark shifting shadows crawling along the corners of the tiled floor. They gathered behind The Pink Cowboy, pulling their way up his body to his ears.

"Do you even know what you want?" The shadows carried and echoed his words around the room in a hushed feverish whisper. "No one does, Theo. There's a seed planted in everyone, and it continues to feast, unwilling to be satisfied." He touched the brim of his hat, resting it back some. "*You* have seen it. *You* have *experienced* it. Your eyes have now been open to the possibilities. What we can offer the world, what we can change about it, is infinite." He reached out his palm, letting it hang frozen in time.

My mind and body were becoming separate, pulled apart. My body sensed the coldness of the room clawing at my skin, while my mind felt the words of The Pink Cowboy seizing my thoughts. The shadows that clung to him rose up and struck through the air taking hold of me.

YEAR: 2032   *DAY: 232 of 232*

EPISODE 93

*There are caves with shadows, and they continue to grow
longer. Is this because the sun is rising?*

I opened the door to the apartment at the top of the stairs.
The darkened tunnel I traversed before it, was just on the
other side of the empty Mind Trap chamber. The air in the
foyer smelled stale and of sweat. When I turned the handle to
enter, I noticed a small sound like a buzzing making its way
into my ear. I believed it to be the Time Guardian.

In the living room, a detective was frozen and eyeballing
me out of the corner of his eye. This amusement would have
stayed with me if it wasn't for turning to see the cyborg man in
which I helped escape and defend from the Monarch prison
system years before. Syfus was a friend, and I immediately
wondered how he became trapped yet again, but this time
with a disparaging man who claimed to be a detective through
the crack of his mouth.

"Be quiet a moment, detective Connolly." I whispered
across the room.

"Bill, you have to save us!" Syfus used all his strength.
His mechanical joints pushed and conjoined its sprockets in
attempt to flee. Tears of pain building up in the crevices of his
eyes.

"Don't struggle." I said, "You'll only make it worse. A Time Guardian has control over this room."

The two of them shook their heads at me, but I knew the presence of the Guardian to be a fact. And I also knew the only way to combat the demon from Cloud Tech.

"I'm going to tell you a story, Syfus. Roger. And I want you to remember that when I tell it, that I am only the vessel and there is another Voice speaking through me to share it. Do you understand?" I took a seat in one of the living room chairs, carefully. They attempted a nod as I sat, but I knew they didn't quite comprehend the complication of this story's telling. Because when you tell a story, it's almost never your own. It involves everything from the outside world that has made an impression on you. Your thoughts turned words on pages or transmitted orally to the world are simply shadows that have yet to be transformed by your light of the story. But before it leaves your mouth, or before the ink spills on the page, it is a truth that almost no one can witness.

The buzzing from the Guardian grew louder as it sensed my sitting down. As skilled as I am in stealth and dexterity, I am still an imperfect vessel of someone else's story. And I hoped, right then, that as I began to mouth the words of the story, that the veil of the Cloud would be lifted so they could control themselves in the apartment again.

YEAR: 2032   **DAY: -3 of 232**

EPISODE 94

The world had gathered around their televisions to watch, earnestly waiting for the event to start as the countdown displayed. Through the pixelated glass box, the numbers dwindled with concentrated ease, maintaining a tension and anticipation felt by its viewers. Their own vanity was hidden from them. White static lines flickered across the screen, as an indiscernible image flashed in repetition.

They told me to wait. That they'd return with his belongings. The engineered clouds gradually spread apart, as the view of the city took their place. Cold grey colors crept over the terrain and encroached into the boardroom where elongated shadows festered in the corners. My continual distrust of these people was beginning to rise. I had always felt anxious being indoors. The outside called to me ever since I was young, feeling more like home than anyplace else. It's where I was most comfortable. But that place was so far removed, unimaginable now. The process of engineering clouds, weather, the sky, the moon, and the sun were all normal. It was all some knew that were born after the Cloud.

In the stillness of the room, a mechanical gear shifted smoothly along the paneled wall. A large flat screen television was revealed in the hidden compartment. It turned on without being prompted. I wondered if the command came from another sector inside the company. Sound and images emerged from the device, while I cautiously checked my surroundings. I tried to command it off, but that didn't work. Static images of serene beaches, isolated wildernesses, and archaic architecture dissolved one after another.

I wish I turned away. The images were all places I've seen before, taken from textbooks, magazines, photos and such. All could have been taken directly from my mind. They appeared exactly how I remember seeing them. Seeing the images again, like this, reminded me of when I first stumbled upon them as if summoning those memories. This effect subconsciously drew me closer towards the device. I hardly noticed my body gravitating towards it when the new image flashed. It was of a bare apartment wall. The color of the wall was a teal shading. In the center where the shadows were converging, I saw a smudge that bubbled and protruded with fungi.

Latching my eyes shut as hard as I could, I fell to my knees trying to fight it. I was brought back to that painful moment again. The things we didn't say to each other. The glass box cast a blue hue onto me, which allowed the rest of the room to fall into darkness. I was being judged.

In my mind's eye there was a faint light being swallowed by the dark. I felt tormented by the pain, by the sadness of it all. Then, I remembered the illusion of the Shadowed Moon. That sign I witnessed of something still out there to reach for. It struck me then. I didn't want to feel this pain, this hurt, this sadness, but they were necessary. Darkness and light; rather to give in to only one, they exist in the balance of awareness, of transformation. I opened my eyes and rose up.

YEAR: 2032   **DAY: 232 of 232**

EPISODE 95

I'm starting to sense the truth. The thing I want has never seemed so close.

I felt crushed stone beneath my feet. A red moon hung above the tracks before the blue-haired devil and I as we abruptly stopped in the dark. It felt like the end of the world. And I kept repeating that melancholy train of thought without any will to stop it. Physically, I gathered I was in a strong trance that was beyond any attempt to break free. I stared across the railway, seeing the cabin resting just below a twisted patch of pine trees.

The door to the cabin opened, giving way to a mirror effect of the red moonlight from the sky to shed a path across the tracks and to the stones under my worn shoes. I heard the faint call of the Conductor. That scruff on his face with bloodshot eyes reminded me of a particular horror film I once watched while both my parents were alive. That same sense of dread and despair made its way into my heart at this moment. A nostalgic recall of memories from my childhood splintered in my mind. And his face was flashing like a film before my eyes.

"You must follow the red light, Clarice. I cannot follow any further." The blue hair shivering in the cold breeze behind me made a whispering flap in the profound darkness. I followed his or the red beam's orders and began to walk to the cabin alone. This was not a dream. I was not in the ethereal space, and not in the Cloud. This place where the Conductor lived was not of Earth, Heaven, Hell or cosmos. But I was told by the frail, old blue-haired man that it was a place where choices are made.

The walk to the door was silent, not even a breeze in the branches of the surrounding pine. I crossed the threshold of the cabin and was immediately greeted by the Conductor's strained stare in the lamplight by his bed. At first glance, it appeared he had no form except a head. But I started to take in my environment and then noticed his bum leg and the cane beside his bed post.

"You're the Conductor?" I questioned out of nervousness. A wicked grin formed on his face. It was an oddly comforting reaction. I expected to be murdered when first entering his neglected home, but I was thinking heavily on every ability I grew to master during my journey to potentially combat-

"You have no power here, Clarice. And there is no one coming to your aid. Sit. We have much to discuss." The Conductor glared out the window of his cabin, and I followed his gaze. I swore on my life that I saw a figure staring back at us from the other side of the pane.

YEAR: 2032   *DAY: -2 of 232*

EPISODE 96

ABSORB AND CONSUME

The words flashed repetitiously on screen between static images of the apartment wall. At first, they were indiscernible. White noise and static blurring their transmission, a subliminal carving emitting through the device. But once identified, it became burned into my irises. Instinct took over. My arm seized a Bankers Lamp and hurled it at the television. The image erupted, sending a bright flash of light into the boardroom as shards of glass flung back towards me. I lingered in the destruction only for a moment.

I knew I didn't have long. An alarm had to have been sent and they'd come for me. I rushed out of the room. Dashing down the hallway past the waiting pods, I saw them filled with people in a paralyzed state of entertained stasis waiting to be seen. Large monitors turned on along the hall one after another, all with the same apartment wall meant for me. I kept running, not allowing my attention to be captured.

A door at the end of the hall opened. Armed guards rifled through it and stood holding electrically charged weapons. Their bodies and faces were completely covered in some form of tech suit and square helmet with rectangular eyepieces.

They retained no distinguishable element of a human underneath their armor. Their movements were unified, as if programmed. I dove into an empty waiting pod and sent the machine spiraling down the chute.

The waiting pod soared down only for a moment before they took control again. A display flashed on and a woman appeared asking to rate my experience at Cloud Tech. I could feel the pod shift, traveling upwards to the top.

When it stopped, I expected to be captured immediately. I would fight and struggle till it led to my death if that would be the case, but when the door opened a long dark hallway lay straight ahead to an emblazoned door. The emblem was a reversible image of a tree. It had long, lush green branches bearing fruit on top. Underneath the dirt, thinly entangled roots twisted in the same pattern of the branches. I bolted forward into the unknown room.

It was quiet, a vacuum of soundlessness. My own movements created no noise. A clap of my hands produced nothing. There were no windows and at the end of the room a compartmental door masked in the wall where a shimmer of daylight shined in. I was on a path that led only one way. There was no turning back, and no escape.

Beyond the door, a set of stairs led me to a latched rooftop entrance. The floor was a glossy coated black marble, completely flat and bare except for a telescope. I could feel the humidity in the air but understood that this was artificially manufactured. Everything in our city was designed and reimagined based on algorithms from what we remembered. My own love of the world, the beautiful creation it once had, was gone. I looked through the telescope and the city below came into view. Buildings full of people complacently sitting, statically staring. I heard the mechanical groove of the latch open behind me. A swarm of guards stood, lined single file, poised to strike.

I gingerly released my grip of the telescope. In that moment, I grew tired of looking through the glass, watching others watch. I took a deep breath, as the guards silently stood in place. Closing my eyes, I silently reflected in thought for no one else to know or observe.

CRAAACK! A booming thunderous sound struck, and the atmosphere encompassing the city cracked like a shard of glass.

YEAR: 2032   **DAY: 232 of 232**

EPISODE 97

The Voice was speaking through me, and I heard what I said to Syfus and Roger. Even after the telling of the story, I still wondered where we were. I posed this question to the two of them. And they told me, in a frozen posture, that this was Clarice's apartment from when she lived in the Monarch city. The realm in which this building now resided was unknown. But it felt like a dream.

It was then the story I told, mixed with the memories I collected in my venture to protect and guide Clarice, came together as means for understanding my purpose. And my purpose is mostly frivolous and I will never see the results in pursuit of it. It is in this revelation that I find joy and melancholy as one in the same. I accept it, and I am compelled to finish it.

I nodded to Syfus and Roger. Their mannequin-like presence made me comfortable to transmit the narrative from the Voice. I explained what it felt like to be a mentor of someone who was not meant for this world. In that explanation there was no mention of regret, but there was of surrender to a destiny for the mentee outside of my comprehension. My creation was put into a strange and perfect world for a transcendental purpose. That purpose was tied to another.

As opposite of a perfect, verbal retelling, I was forced

to pause. The Time Guardian materialized in the form of a gargantuan fly, and it suspended itself by flapping its wings in a manipulated slowing of speed. Its two bulbous eyes were the first feature the three of us noticed at once. The compound eye staring at us, unmoving but watching without ceasing. The creature was without a doubt a god of this unknowable realm, and it had our undivided attention.

The Time Guardian spoke in a language that once heard was immediately related to the strings section of an orchestra. But between what we heard through our ears, the words solidified and were translated for our understanding. "You're here for the ending of one path, but there is another." The giant fly in the room became engulfed in a thick black smoke that was horrific at first, but then subsided. We awaited any further communication.

One of its legs extended and its claw pointed past us to the sliding glass door of Clarice's apartment balcony. The crimson residue, that had been there the whole time, was aged and rotting within its small circumference on the pane. "The smudge is a timeless thing for this world. Be thankful for its creation," the fly whispered. And then it disappeared. That's when the glass door slid open.

YEAR: 2032   **DAY: -1 of 232**

EPISODE 98

The path has been leading towards this exchange. The decisions I've made bear the faint resemblance of choicelessness, feeling more like suggestions or a dream where the freedom of choice doesn't matter when approaching two shut doors. Whichever one you open, ultimately is guided by the dreamer and the subconscious.

There is a beginning, middle, and end to the crimson-tinted room where I stand, immobilized by the emollient breeze and the howling shadows. Both forces encircle me into a stasis rigid posture as The Pink Cowboy's index finger is primed, aimed at me. The beginning of the room lies in front and is marked by the chair and fish tank, and just beyond it a door with an emblazoned pattern of a tree. The end of the room lies behind me, covered in twisting shadows carrying whispering cries and voices in its great obscure depth. The gradient of crimson light guides my eye from one side to the other.

"Have a drink, Theo." He said, producing a dark brown liquor in a cocktail glass from his hand and extending it towards me, "Relax, so we can talk." His voice was as smooth as what I imaged the bourbon he held tasted like. I said nothing but took another moment to look around the room. "Not thirsty anymore?" His eyes raised slightly astonished. "How bout a cigar?" And just like that, he now held a thick Cuban cigar where the drink once was. It was lit, but the ember was hidden, much like the upper part of his face behind the brim of his hat. I closed my eyes, concentrating on my breath, on my thoughts, trying to figure a way out. "Help me out, Theo. There's no escape. Why not indulge in a little talk? What do you want? What is it I can offer you?" He said.

"Nothing," I said in a sharp-toned whisper. "I want freedom, choices, none of which Cloud Tech or *you* offer." The *tick* resurfaced somewhere deep in my mind. It was an insurmountable pressure building, almost as if a blunt jagged object was being pushed into the back of my head.

"No one has choices anymore, Theo. Only the illusion of choice exists. That's part of the beauty of what we've built here though, wouldn't you agree? As long as the illusion exists, people are satisfied because they think they're making a choice out of free-will. Even before the illusion, people didn't want to choose. They wanted options, suggestions. Consider it a starting place or a branch to jump from. Bear with me a moment." He moved across the room as the atmosphere pushed and pulled like water around him. "Consider the television writer. They're coming up with a new show. Now, how they make that choice might have something to do with analytics of viewers' interests. A culmination of data predicts a series of shows that *a majority* would watch, *but* they aren't consciously looking for currently. It's only after they're given the option that they realize that's exactly what they wanted. The system has proven its use. Now, imagine *if* we had access to personal memories, and from there we have our *branch*. We build a narrative that makes the viewing experience more personalized, even resonating to the unbeknownst *watcher*. We don't force the viewer to watch, they still have a choice whether to tune in or not. And that, my friend, is the magic trick. The illusion has been created."

His over-exaggerated movements carried a theatrical flair. Hidden within his words I felt a realization form in me. The grip of the shadows released me, and I was free to move again and make my own choices. I thought of the surreal dreams Laura use to have, the strange ability to create within them through lucid dreaming, as compared to my own. In my dreams I often was guided with a lack of choice. It unfolded as I followed a path, that path often *illuminated by the light*. In the room I looked at the door, the lit path. I had no idea what laid beyond it. Turning back towards the shadows, there was the end of the line. I stepped forward, engulfed by the darkness.

"Interesting choice, Theo." The Pink Cowboy's words carried through the waves of the shadow, stinging my ears. Fumbling around, I couldn't see anything, *but* I couldn't be seen. The Pink Cowboy's taunts and temptations continued, feeling closer and closer with each ticking second. His words landed like a subtle breath on my neck.

My hands were outstretched, reaching and grasping for anything. The shadows remained thick and danced around my body. Closing my eyes, I concentrated, listening for the feeling. I've always been a man of sight and science, of numbers and equations, and in that moment, I released it all, allowing my body to feel the space and freedom from the Shadows. The *tick* finally released me. My hand reached a smooth object almost instantly. I opened my eyes, which revealed a screen that showed Laura standing on a roof lined by armed guards. She lay just beyond the glass. I heard the voice of The Pink

Cowboy in my ear and felt the Shadows crawl up my skin. The glass provided the final illusion. This viewing experience was meant for me. I sent my balled fist into the glass, then again, and again, until it finally splintered and cracked.

YEAR: 2032   **DAY: 232 of 232**

EPISODE 99

The greatest fear a finite being should have is that its memory would be erased and that history would be altered to a point of being rewritten. Do we choose to remember, no matter the amount of pain?

I was bound to a chair. My head felt like it was splitting, being filled with too much information to comprehend or to discern. The Conductor sat motionless on his cot, keeping us in a locked stare. The amount of knowledge was separating my mind from my heart. I began to panic, convulse, and cry.

"What is it that you want, Clarice?" The Conductor coughed. "You cannot stay in my realm. You won't survive." I blinked to cast out those words that he transmitted to me telepathically. Immediately following that blink, my environment was changed. I was now sitting in a steel chair, in the doctor's office. Upon my head was the helmet. The scanning was manipulating my neurons, searing my synapses. I was shaking, teeth chattering, and tongue flailing in and out of my mouth.

I blinked again, fighting every thought as it was forced into my mind's eye. Memories, dreams, and knowledge of the known world were rushed into view. Overload accompanied by a loud beeping, and the squealing of the doctor's swivel chair. My eyes felt like they were bleeding past my eyelids. From the pupil, through the lens, hitting my retina. Then, silence. I was no longer trapped in a chair. My eyes closed; I felt the warmth of the sun on my back.

I was many stories up, standing on the balcony of my old apartment, which now felt new to me. My back was to the city as I gazed upon a blurred sheet of glass that made up the sliding door to the inside. I could see the indistinct shape of someone on the other side of the glass. I became short of breath, anxious. So, I opened the sliding glass door to be greeted by an empty living room, but in a clarity I've never experienced before.

Walking in, I sensed the warmth of a life truly lived in this place. The silence of the room was invigorating and calming. I shifted to the kitchen, noticing a sketch pad on the island counter. I opened it, flipping slowly through each page from the beginning. Character after character: a trainer in harem pants, holding a staff. A young Cyborg with a kind face sharing similarity to my own facial features. A rugged Captain with a devilish grin. And the last page depicted a noir detective in a trench coat, seeming tired and confused. *I must've drawn these*, I thought to myself.

I found myself daydreaming of these characters, feeling less alone in the empty apartment. That daydreaming led to a familiar drowsiness. And so, I moved to the couch across from the wall television. I feel asleep on the couch and immediately awoke. A voice came from the kitchen behind me in a cautious whisper. "Clarice, what do you want," my mother asked. I turned just enough to see her silhouetted figure through my peripherals. I laid there, eyes wide open, mind clear. I said, "I want to live a life that has yet to be written."

YEAR: Unknown   **DAY: 1**

EPISODE 100

"Hunger is a *mean* thing." B.W. Wuxler sat staring at a diminished, droopy, and confused face, one of complete sadness of spirit. He dwelled on his sayings which brought back the memories and his own conscious sadness. "Hunger *is a mean thing.*" The words choked out of him, giving him pause, hanging in the depths of his throat, as an excess of spittle and bodily fluids formed in his mouth, nose and eyes. He was the eldest and senior member of the Wuxler family. Looking down at his amputated limbs hanging from the end of the wheelchair he kept recalling, welcoming and bringing back *knowing* pain which existed in his memories. "Men don't cry, they don't share things with their sons. They don't— Where was I?" His eyes and mind raced. "Korea." He patted his limbs tenderly, as if it were a sacrifice for the betterment. "We-we grew up hungry. We didn't have much food. We had a potato farm, and if the crops didn't grow, we didn't eat. I know what a mean thing hunger is. Let me tell you—" B.W. coughed, it was a deep brutish cough from years of tobacco use that now caused tar-filled lungs. He regained the shallow, still breaths that have become regular for him at his deteriorating age. "Let me tell you about Korea, when I was there in the military, fighting. War is a mean thing, not just cause of what it does to the ones fighting, but because of what it does to the people who have to endure through the fighting as it goes on around them. They were all hungry there, the kids. Brittle as a twig. I'd go through the chow hall and only eat *half my plate*. I'd take the other half outside and throw it in the garbage and watch as kids—" B.W. couldn't hold back the tears, which came flowing out as his voice broke "-as the kids would come up and dig through it and eat *from my plate*." B.W.'s head dropped, and so did the diminished, droopy, and confused face. At the Wuxler Gala, B.W. Wuxler was positioned in the corner of the room, far from anyone else, talking to his own reflection.

Most of the Wuxler family members suffered, in some form, from what might be described as *empatheia-phobia*. "I'm starving, will the caterer be arriving, Wallaby?" Winnipeg stated in a sharp, brute tone, one that sounded rhetorical and eluded to an indirect insult, because she knew, just like the rest of the family suspected, that Wallaby was incapable of handling one responsibility and thus had prepared ahead of time with a backup caterer who was currently stuck in bumper to bumper traffic on the freeway and would not be attending this evening. "I don't know, they should be here by now." Wallaby said munching on a *Cheese Blitz* snack he had tucked away in his pocket in case of emergencies. He had more but didn't tell anyone. The caterer Wallaby hired (yes, he did in fact hire one) was not present yet, which is not really true because the caterer had shown up before anyone got there, and because they were the caterer the year prior knew what a pain the Wuxler family presented. The caterer, instead of setting up, found a way into the rafters of the building and laid out the trays of food they'd prepared. It was an elaborate setup, but they sat watching the event from above while feasting on the spread, as fans blew the smells through the vents and down below. "I must be losing my mind. I could swear I smell lamb!" Winnipeg exclaimed. Someone else said they smelled roast duck, another one said they smelled fish, while someone else vociferously said, with a pretentious finger raised and confident air aboding them, they smelled something "exotic", which Winnipeg responded, your smeller is bad, all while the caterer in the rafters belly laughed as his plan seemed to be working quite well, until a piece of fish bone got lodged in his throat.

The Wuxler gala took place in the Charlie Chapel, owned and named by Bjorn Wuxler on their own private island and the event was televised to the world in a grand showcase but had not yet been streaming live. The countdown displayed properly on an extravagant projector and was ticking down, as all groups of people around the world had gathered around the television sets next to home-cooked meals, microwavable suppers, and restaurant-based dinners to watch. The event, held every year, was prestigious and renowned, and because the food every year was the biggest deal of all, the Wuxlers' often skipped eating anything for the day to make room for the elegant feast they were all so expecting. The countdown ticked down, seconds away from going live to the room filled with hungry creative thinkers, who could only think about their empty stomachs. Wuxler members snapped at each other, ferociously reprimanding one another as their family feuds boiled to a maximum. Wallaby looked towards the projector watching the numbers tick away and saw brief flashes of the words *ABSORB AND CONSUME* between the static. "Does anyone else see that?" No one else did, all remained unobservant, except for Wallaby. The room fell into a silent glare and gurgling stomachs.

So now then, there was B.W. sitting contemplatively staring at his own painful remembrances, there was the caterer in the rafters whose bluing face attempted to draw his last breath, there was Winnipeg who snatched the *Cheese Blitz* from Wallaby, but in pride refused to take a bite, instead dropping it to the floor stomping on it, there was Wallaby who was scolded by each family member and left the room dejected finding the bare of sustenance stainless-steel kitchen where he stumbled upon a pallet of expired chocolate pudding, and there was the people watching their televisions with eager anticipation for the event which finally started, and all of them, every last one of them attending, watching and listening, remained *hungry* for something more.

YEAR: 2033   **DAY: The Day of the Wuxler Gala**

ABOUT THE AUTHORS

Jonathan Wymer was born in St. Louis, Missouri. He now resides in Atlanta, Georgia with his wife and pug.

Joshua Messarge was born in Trenton, New Jersey. He now resides in Atlanta, Georgia.

ACKNOWLEDGEMENTS

I would like to thank my wife, Lisa. With your patience and kindness, I was able to write a story that is mostly patient and kind. To my parents, you are the storytellers who shaped every frame of my imagination and are undoubtedly the most insightful beings on the planet. And to my siblings, who will never know how much they inspire me.

- *Jonathan Wymer*

A very special thanks to Carrie Prescott for generously giving her time to read this work. Thank you to a long list of people who have inspired and encouraged me along the road, I'm so thankful to know you all. Thank you Nauna for all too much.

- *Joshua Messarge*

Made in the USA
Columbia, SC
27 May 2021

38547941R00140